Bingo Brown and the
Language of Love

ALSO BY BETSY BYARS

After the Goat Man
The Burning Questions of Bingo Brown
The Cartoonist
Cracker Jackson
The Cybil War
The 18th Emergency
The Glory Girl
Go and Hush the Baby
The House of Wings
The Midnight Fox
The Summer of the Swans
Trouble River
The TV Kid

BETSY BYARS

Bingo Brown and the Language of Love

VIKING KESTREL

Drawings by Cathy Bobak

VIKING KESTREL
Published by the Penguin Group
Viking Penguin, a division of Penguin Books USA Inc.,
40 West 23rd Street, New York, New York 10010, U.S.A.
Penguin Books Ltd, 27 Wrights Lane, London W8 5TZ, England
Penguin Books Australia Ltd, Ringwood, Victoria, Australia
Penguin Books Canada Ltd, 2801 John Street, Markham, Ontario, Canada L3R 1B4
Penguin Books (N.Z.) Ltd, 182–190 Wairau Road, Auckland 10, New Zealand
Penguin Books Ltd, Registered Offices: Harmondsworth, Middlesex, England

First published in 1989 by Viking Penguin, a division of Penguin Books USA Inc.
Published simultaneously in Canada
1 3 5 7 9 10 8 6 4 2
Copyright © Betsy Byars, 1989
All rights reserved

Library of Congress Cataloging-in-Publication Data
Byars, Betsy Cromer.   Bingo Brown and the language of love
by Betsy Byars.   p.   cm.
Summary: As fifth grader Bingo Brown strives for the triumphs of today and
steels himself against the tribulations of tomorrow, he discovers that he
will have to undergo a few more trials and triumphs before growing up.
ISBN 0-670-82791-6   I. Title.   PZ7.B9836Bi 1989   [Fic]—dc19
69-30224   AC

Printed in the United States of America
Set in Sabon Roman

Contents

Bingo Brown and the Language of Love

The Groundhog Mustache

Every time Bingo Brown smelled gingersnaps, he wanted to call Melissa long distance.

Actually, it was more of a burning desire than a want, Bingo decided. One minute ago he had been standing here, smiling at himself in the bathroom mirror, when without any warning he had caught a whiff of ginger. Now he had to call Melissa. Had to!

"Are you still admiring yourself?" his mom asked as she passed the door.

"Mom, come here a minute."

His mom leaned in the doorway.

"Is that a mustache on my face or what?"

"Dirt."

"Mom, you didn't even look."

"Do your lip like that."

Obediently Bingo stretched his upper lip down over his teeth.

His mom said, "Ah, yes, I was right the first time—dirt."

"Mom, it's not dirt. It's hair. There may be dirt on the hair but . . ." He leaned closer to the mirror. "I would be the first student in Roosevelt Middle School to have a mustache."

"Supper!" his dad called from the kitchen. His dad was stir-frying tonight.

"A lot of women would be thrilled to have a son with a mustache," Bingo said, "though I'll have to shave before I go to high school. You aren't allowed to have mustaches in high school."

Bingo moved away from the mirror, still watching himself. "You can't see it from here, but"—he stepped closer—"from right here, it's definitely a premature mustache."

"Bingo, supper's ready." His mother picked up a bill as she went through the living room.

Bingo followed quickly. "Hey, Dad," he said. "Notice anything different about me?"

His father turned—he was holding the wok in both hands—but before he could spy the mustache, Bingo's mom interrupted. "You will not believe the trouble I'm having with the telephone company."

Bingo's father said, "Oh?" He put down the wok and wiped his hands on his apron before taking the bill.

"Can you believe that? They're trying to tell me that somebody in this family made fifty-four dollars and twenty-nine cents worth of calls to a place called Bixby, Oklahoma."

Bingo gasped. He caught the door to keep from falling to his knees.

"Fifty-four dollars and twenty-nine cents! I told the phone company, 'Nobody in this family knows anybody in the whole state of Oklahoma, much less Bixby.' Bixby!"

Bingo said, "Mom—"

"The woman obviously did not believe me. Where does the telephone company get these idiots? I said to her, 'Are you calling me a liar?' She said, 'Now, Madame—' "

Bingo said, "Mom—"

"Wait till I'm through talking to your father, Bingo."

"This can't wait," Bingo said.

"Bingo, if it's about your invisible mustache—"

"It's n-not. I wish it were," he said, stuttering a little.

Bingo's mom sighed with impatience. Bingo knew that she got a lot of pleasure from a righteous battle with a big company and must hate his interruption. He hated it himself.

"So?" she said. "Be quick."

Bingo cleared his throat. He walked into the room in the heavy-footed way he walked in his dreams. He clutched the back of his chair for support.

"Remember Melissa—that girl that used to be in my room at school?"

"Yes, Bingo, get on with it."

"M-member I said she moved?" he was reverting back to the way he talked when he was a child.

"No, I don't, but go on."

"You have to remember! You and Dad drove me over to say good-bye! It was Grammy's birthday!"

"Yes, I remember that she moved. What about it, Bingo? Get on with it."

"Well, she m-moved to Oklahoma."

"Bixby, Oklahoma?"

Bingo nodded.

There was a long silence while his parents looked at him. The moment stretched like a rubber band. Before it snapped, Bingo cleared his throat to speak.

His mom beat him to it. "Are you telling me," she said in a voice that chilled his bones, "that you made"—she whipped the bill from his father's fingers and consulted it—"seven calls"—now she looked at him again—"for a total of"—eyes back to the bill—"fifty-four dollars and twenty-nine cents"—eyes back to him—"to this person in Bixby, Oklahoma?"

"She's not a person! She's Melissa! Anyway, Mom, you knew she had moved. I showed you the picture postcard she sent me."

"I thought she'd moved across town."

"She drew the postcard herself. I'll get it and show it to you if you don't believe me. It said 'Greetings from Bixby, OK.' Her address was there, and her phone number.

"As soon as I got the postcard, I went into the living room. You were sitting on the sofa, studying for your real estate license. I showed you the postcard and asked you if I could call Melissa."

He was now clutching the back of the chair the way old people clutch walkers.

"My exact words were, 'Would it be all right if I called Melissa?' Your exact words were, 'Yes, but don't make a pest of yourself.' That's why the calls were so short, Mom. I didn't want to make a pest of myself!"

His mother was still looking at the bill. "I cannot believe this. Fifty-four dollars and twenty-nine cents worth of calls to Bixby, Oklahoma."

"I'm sorry, Mom. It was just a misunderstanding."

"I'll say."

"I should have explained it was long distance."

"I'll say."

Bingo's father said, "Well, it's done. Can we eat?" He glanced at the wok with a sigh. "Dinner's probably ruined."

"I don't see how you can eat when we owe the phone company fifty-four dollars and twenty-nine cents," Bingo's mother said.

"I can always eat."

"May I remind you that I have not actually gotten one single commission yet?"

"You may remind me. Now can we eat?"

In a sideways slip Bingo moved around the back of his chair and sat. He began to breathe again.

"Mom, can I ask one question?" Bingo asked, encouraged by the fact that his mother was sitting down, too.

"What?"

"Promise you won't get mad."

"I'm already furious. Just being mad would be a wonderful relief."

"Well, promise you won't get any madder."

"What is the question, Bingo?"

"Can I make one more call to Melissa? Just one? You can take it out of my allowance."

"What do you think?" she asked.

"Mom, it's important. I need to tell her why I won't be calling anymore."

"Bingo, when you put fifty-four dollars and twenty-nine cents into my hand, then we'll talk about telephone calls. Until then you are not to make any calls whatsoever. You are not to touch the telephone. Understood?"

"Understood."

"Now eat."

"I'm really not terribly hungry."

"Eat anyway."

Bingo helped himself to the stir-fry. The smell of ginger was overpowering now. It was coming from the wok! No wonder he was being driven mad. And if the mere scent of ginger had this effect on him—it was at the moment twining around his head, pulling him like a noose toward the phone—what would the taste do to him? Would he run helplessly to the phone? Would he dial? Would he cry hoarsely to Melissa of his passion while his parents looked on in disgust?

Bingo broke off. He had promised to give up burning questions for the summer, cold turkey, but how could he do that when questions blazed like meteors across the sky of his mind? When they—

"Eat!"

Bingo put a small piece of chicken into his mouth. The taste of ginger, fortunately, did not live up to its smell.

As he swallowed, he rubbed his fingers over his upper lip. The mustache—as he had known it would be—was gone. It had come out like the groundhog, seen its shadow in the glare of his mom's anger, and done the sensible thing—made a U-turn and gone back underground.

After supper Bingo went to his room and pulled out his summer notebook. There were two headings in the notebook. One was "Trials of Today." Under that, Bingo now listed:

1. Parental misunderstanding of a mere phone bill and, more importantly, their total disregard and concern for the depth of my feeling for Melissa.

2. Disappearance of a beloved mustache and the accompanying new sensation of manliness.

3. Breaking my vow to give up burning questions for the summer.

4. Tasting ginger, which, while it did not drive me as mad as I had feared, has left me with a bad case of indigestion.

The second heading was "Triumphs of Today." Under that Bingo wrote only one word: none.

A Knock at the Window

"Dear Melissa,"

Bingo lay on his Smurf sheets. He had always been able to count on a peaceful night's sleep on his Smurf sheets. But last Tuesday Billy Wentworth had come over, looked at his unmade bed, and smiled condescendingly at the Smurfs. After that, Bingo had not been easy on them.

Right now he was as uncomfortable as if he were lying on real Smurfs. However, he knew tonight was not a good time to ask his mother for more manly sheets.

He glanced at his letter and read what he had written.

"Dear Melissa,"

He retraced the comma and stared up at the ceiling.

Writing Melissa was not the same as calling her, because as soon as she heard his voice, she always said something like, "Oh, Bingo, it's you! That's exactly who I was hoping it would be."

Her voice would actually change, get warmer somehow,

deeper with pleasure. Girls were fortunate to have high voices so they could deepen them so effectively. His own voice got higher when he was pleased, which wasn't a good effect at all.

If his mom only knew how it made a man feel to hear a girl's voice deepen with pleasure. He knew there was no point in trying to explain that to his mom. His mom was in no mood to understand.

After supper, he had asked her for a stamp, one measly stamp, and she had said, "I'll sell you one."

"Sell?"

"Yes, sell." She walked to the desk, tore one stamp off the roll, and held it out. Her other hand was out, too, palm up. "That'll be twenty-five cents."

"Mom!"

"One quarter, please."

Then he had to go through the indignity of borrowing a quarter from his father.

And after all that humiliation, he couldn't seem to get the letter started.

"Dear Melissa,"

He changed the comma to a semicolon.

"Dear Melissa;"

As he lay there, he thought of that terrible, heart-stopping moment when he had learned Melissa was moving.

It had been a spring day. Mr. Mark, their teacher, was back after his motorcycle accident. He walked with a cane, but there was the general feeling in the classroom that everything was back to normal at last and things would go well for the rest of the year.

Bingo was at the pencil sharpener, grinding down a pencil, admiring the April day, when Melissa stood up behind him.

Bingo had not heard the snap of pencil lead, but his pulse quickened because he thought Melissa was going to join him. He and Melissa had had pleasant, even thrilling, pencil sharpener encounters before.

He turned toward her with an encouraging smile. Melissa was standing stiffly by her desk, arms at her side. She said, "Mr. Mark?"

"Yes, Melissa."

"May I make an announcement?"

"Can't it wait a bit? Some people are still working on their journals."

Melissa's eyes filled with tears. She started to sit down, and Mr. Mark reconsidered. "Gang, is anyone working so hard on his or her journal that their train of thought would be shattered forever by an announcement from Melissa?" His bright eyes looked them over. "Melissa, it's all yours."

"This is a personal announcement. Is that all right?"

He nodded.

Bingo's heart had moved up into his throat. As soon as he had seen the tears, he had started closing the distance between them. He and Melissa were now two feet apart, close enough so that Bingo could see her tears were getting ready to spill.

Bingo could stand tears if they stayed where they were supposed to, but if they spilled . . .

"My dad," Melissa said. She looked down at her desk

and blinked her eyes. Two tears plopped onto her open journal.

Bingo gasped with concern.

"My father," she began again with brave determination, "is being transferred to Bixby, Oklahoma, and we'll be moving next month. I hope some of you will write to me. That's the end of my announcement."

Melissa sat down, but Bingo stood there. He vowed with silent fervor to write daily, and to write such letters as the post office had never seen, letters so thick postal workers would marvel at their weight. His letters would go down in postal history. Years later, an unusually thick letter would be referred to as a "Bingo letter." His letters—

"Bingo?"

"What? Oh, yes, Mr. Mark?"

"Melissa said that was the end of her announcement. I believe you might begin to think in terms of returning to your seat."

"I'm on my way."

That memory caused Bingo to pick up his pen with renewed determination.

"Well," he wrote firmly, "I guess you're surprised to be getting a letter from me instead of a call, but our telephone bill came today."

There was a knock on his window. Bingo leaped in alarm. No one had ever knocked on his window before. He was as shocked as if someone had knocked on his forehead.

He got to his feet. Whoever was doing the knocking was either incredibly stupid or incredibly impolite!

Bingo strode to the window and bent down. The reflection of his own face, frowning, was all he could see.

"Who's out there?" Bingo asked. "Didn't your mother ever teach you not to knock on—"

"It's me, Worm Brain."

Bingo swallowed the rest of his words.

"Open up."

"Oh, all right." Bingo opened the window and looked at Billy Wentworth. Billy was wearing his camouflage T-shirt and his Rambo expression. "What can I do for you?" Bingo asked.

"Why can't you talk on the phone?"

"Who says I can't?"

"Your mom. I called and asked to speak to you, and she said, 'Bingo is no longer allowed to receive calls.' Bam! She could have busted my eardrum. You being punished?"

"Unjustly," Bingo said.

"Is there any other way? What'd you do?"

"I ran up a fifty-four-dollar phone bill," Bingo said. "So, why did you knock on my window?"

"I wanted to ask you something. Well, my mom wanted me to ask you something."

"What?"

"We're going on vacation and we can't take our dog."

"Misty the poodle?" Bingo asked.

A feeling of dread began deep within Bingo's soul. Before Misty had moved next door, Bingo had not known it was possible to actually dread being stared at by a dog.

"Mom, she stares at me all the time, right into my eyes."

"That's known as eye contact," his mom had said, in her usual unconcerned way.

"And I don't know what she wants me to do. Mom, she can stare for hours. Sometimes I have to go in the house!"

"You better get used to eye contact," his mom had said. "Later on you'll be having eye contact with girls, and if you run in the house then, you've blown it."

"Yes," Billy Wentworth went on, "Misty the poodle. How many dogs you think we got, Worm Brain?"

"That's the only one I know about."

"You want to keep her?" Billy asked.

"Well, I don't know. We're probably going on vacation, too."

"Go ask your mom."

"Er, I think she's in the bathroom just—"

"No, she's in the living room. I saw her through the window."

Bingo went into the living room. "We can't keep Misty, can we?"

His mother glanced up. "The Wentworth dog? Sure, why not?"

Bingo lowered his voice. "Mom, you know I can't stand to be stared at by that dog. She—"

"You ought to be ashamed of yourself, Bingo Brown, to mind being looked at by a ten-year-old half-blind miniature poodle with kidney trouble!"

Bingo stood in silence. Up until the business of the phone bill, Bingo and his mother had been getting along unusually well. His mother had a new job selling real estate, and even though she hadn't gotten a commission yet, she was very happy.

"Tell Billy yes!" she went on forcefully. "Tell Billy we

will be glad to keep the poodle. Certainly it will make up, in part, for their having to keep you last fall."

This last humiliation, being put in the category of a dog, made Bingo turn—he hoped with dignity—and start back to his room.

He went directly to Billy, at the open window. "Yes," he said. He closed the window and went back to his bed.

Well, at least he now had something to write to Melissa. "Billy Wentworth's poodle, Misty, will be spending next week with me, so this will probably be my last letter for a while. I'll have to keep an eye on her. Sincerely, but somewhat despondently, Bingo Brown"

He fumbled under the bed for his summer notebook and flipped to "Trials of Today." He wrote:

1. Continued animosity from my mother and the cruel implication that I am, socially, on the same level with a poodle.

2. Having the privacy of my bedroom invaded by an enemy agent.

3. Inability to create postal history by writing Bingo letters to Melissa.

4. Continued failure in reaching the mainstream of life.

It made Bingo feel somewhat better to have survived four trials of this magnitude, but he still had only one word to list under "Triumphs": none.

Chef Bingo

Bingo tied on his apron and looked down at the cookbook on the counter. It was open to page forty-four: chicken breasts in tarragon sauce.

Bingo cracked his knuckles, cheflike.

"Let's see," he said. Beneath his breath, he began to read the ingredients. "Chicken breasts—I have those. Onions—I have those. . . ."

In order to make up for his phone debt, Bingo had agreed to cook supper for his mom and dad for thirty-six nights. His mom had originally wanted fifty-four. "That's fair, Bingo," she had argued, "a dollar a night." But he had bargained her up to a dollar and a half.

"All right, thirty-six," she'd said finally. "But no Hamburger Helper, Bingo."

"Of course not."

This was Bingo's third supper, and he was ready for something from the spice rack. As he rummaged through the little scented tins, he caught the aroma of ginger, but with a quick glance of regret at the telephone, he continued to rummage.

"Tarragon . . . tarragon. I wonder if that's anything like oregano? Garlic . . . dill . . .

"What else do I need to do? Oven"—Bingo turned on the oven with a flourish—"three-fifty." Bingo had already learned that 350 degrees was the perfect cooking temperature. He never planned to use anything else. For example, this tarragon chicken thing called for—he checked the recipe—275, but—

The phone rang and Bingo moved sideways toward it. Bingo was now allowed to answer the phone, but he couldn't place any calls. With his eyes on the cookbook, he picked up the phone.

"Hello."

A voice said, "Could I speak to Bingo, please."

It was a girl's voice!

Bingo was so shocked he almost dropped the phone. He had not spoken to a girl on the phone since his last call to Melissa. He did not think he would ever speak to a girl again.

Now not only was he going to speak to a girl, but it was a strange girl.

A rash of questions burned out of control in his brain. Why was a strange girl calling him? What did she want? He was too young for magazine subscriptions, wasn't he? Could she be conducting a survey? Could it be a woman with a little girl voice wanting him to contribute to a good cause? Could it be—

"Is this Bingo?"

"Well, this is Bingo Brown," he said, emphasizing his last name.

That was quick thinking. After all, there might be other Bingos. He didn't want to proceed with the conversation only to have it end with something like, "Well, boo, I thought I was talking to Bingo Schwartznecker."

"Oh, Bingo. Hi!"

There was a faint tinge of that long-remembered deepening of pleasure. How did girls do that? Did they have two sets of vocal cords, one for everyday use and one for special occasions? Did they shift gears like a car and their motor actually—

"Bingo," she went on in a more businesslike voice, "You don't know me, but my name's Cici, with two *i*'s."

"Oh?"

Bingo's free hand had begun to twitch nervously, as if it wanted to make some sort of gesture but was unsure what the gesture should be.

Bingo put his hand firmly into his apron pocket.

"Cici Boles."

"Oh."

"I'm a good friend of Melissa's, you know? I lived next door to her. But you probably don't recognize my name because I'm not in your grade."

"Oh."

"I'm the same age as Melissa, but I started school in Georgia, and you have to already be, like, five to start kindergarten in Georgia. . . . Are you still there?"

"Yes." At least, Bingo thought, he had broken his string of *oh*s.

"Because I, like, panic when people don't answer me. I think they've gone. I think I'm talking to, you know, empty air!"

"I'm still here."

"Then answer me."

"I will."

"You're probably wondering why I called."

This time Bingo answered as quickly as a bride. "I do."

"You're going to think this is silly, Bingo, but promise you won't hang up on me."

"I promise."

Bingo switched hands, putting his telephone hand—it had started twitching now—into his pocket.

"Well, here goes. Melissa wants me to take a picture of you with my camera and send it to her. See, I knew you'd think it was silly."

Bingo breathed deeply. This was the last thing he had expected, that a girl would want to take his picture. Even his own parents never particularly wanted to take his picture, and now this! A mixed-sex photography session!

"Are you still there?" Cici asked.

"Yes."

"See, you have to answer or I panic. Like, he's gone! I am talking to empty air!"

"Actually, I was thinking."

"Oh, I never stop to do that. I just, you know, go for it. What were you thinking?"

"Er, when do you want to take this picture?"

"Would right now be too soon?"

"Right now?" Bingo bent down to check his reflection in the toaster oven.

"Yes."

Bingo reached for his apron strings. He untied them in a flourish.

"I'll need a few minutes."

"Sure."

Bingo wondered if there was any mousse in the house. He hadn't used mousse since Melissa moved. He had given it up in a sort of religious way, like for Lent.

But if he didn't use it now, Melissa might not recognize him. Worse, she might think he had gotten ugly!

"Better make that fifteen minutes," Bingo told Cici Boles.

He turned off the oven and ran for the bathroom.

As he ran, heart pumping in a way it had not pumped in months, Bingo had burning questions.

Could this mixed-sex photography session turn out to be my first Triumph of Today? Or, more likely, will it be just another Trial?

Will there be mousse?

Is a Triumph possible without mousse?

With hands that trembled, Bingo opened the medicine cabinet. "Ah," he sighed, "mousse." And he reached for the can.

Worm Brain's Picture

Bingo was at the window, watching for Cici Boles. He was getting unhappier by the minute.

Bingo was not ready for another mixed-sex conversation. He had realized this when he was moussing his hair. He hadn't had one in such a long time that he wasn't sure he even remembered how.

Plus the fact that the only good mixed-sex conversations were those with Melissa. When you had a mixed-sex conversation with Melissa, it was like the Olympics of mixed-sex conversations.

This mixed-sex conversation might be mercifully brief.

"Smile."

"Like this?"

"Yes."

Click.

"Thank you."

"Anytime."

But still, with girls you could never tell. This Cici Boles might come up with something like, "By the way, are you doing anything Friday night?"

This thought made his heart throw itself against the wall of his chest, as if to escape.

"By the way, are you doing anything Friday night?" was exactly the kind of mixed-sex conversation he wasn't up to. Probably never would be.

He glanced at his watch. Was it too late to cancel? "Hello, Cici, this is Bingo Brown." No. No! "This is Bingo Brown's brother, and Bingo has been called out of town unexpectedly and—"

Bingo gasped. He leaned forward. A bicycle was coming down the street. There was a girl on the bike!

No, Bingo decided, putting one hand over his racing heart, this girl was much too big and too blond to be Cici. This girl was more like a high school girl—no, make that a college girl. This girl even had—

Bingo gasped again. There was a camera around the big blond's neck.

Bingo ran back to the kitchen so she wouldn't see him peering out the glass. When the bell rang, he walked in a brisk, businesslike manner to the door.

She said, "Well, here I am. I'm Cici."

Bingo said, "So you are."

He attempted to put his hands in his apron pockets, but his apron was back in the kitchen. He slid his hands sideways into his jeans pockets.

"I'll have to take the picture outside," Cici said, "because, you know, I don't have a flash. Is that all right?"

"Yes."

"Front or back?"

Bingo smiled slightly. "Perhaps you should take it from the front so Melissa can see my face. Otherwise, she might not recognize me."

"Oh, Bingo." Cici blinked rapidly. "I meant front yard or backyard."

"Just a little humor," Bingo mumbled.

"Oh, I get it. . . . front . . . back." With one finger—this was awkward because she had long, long nails—she pointed to her front and then her back. "Melissa told me how funny you are."

She might be as big and blond as a college girl, but that was where the similarity ended, Bingo thought. "Back-yard," he said firmly.

In silence, Bingo led the way through the living room, the kitchen, past his apron and the half-skinned chicken breasts, out the back door.

"Oh, let's do it over here by the fence," Cici said. "The roses make a nice background. Melissa's the kind that couldn't care less about the background. She just wants a picture of you. I'm the kind that always likes to do my best."

Bingo stood stiffly against the rosebush, with his hands in his pockets. He said quickly, "How's this?"

"It's fine, but I'm not in focus yet."

"Go ahead and take it," he said through tight lips. He'd only been smiling for a short time, but the day was so hot his teeth were dry.

"There! I've almost got it."

Why had he let this happen? Bingo wondered. Here he was with the sun in his eyes, smelling of mousse, while important chicken breasts waited to be skinned in the kitchen.

Well, he understood now man's weakness for having his picture made. He was living proof of it. The trouble with living proofs was that you actually had to become the living proof before you—

A voice from the other side of the hedge said, "Hey, Worm Brain, is that you over there?"

It was Billy Wentworth!

Bingo pulled back into the rosebush. Thorns raked his arms, but he did not feel the sting. He wanted to pull the branches around him like a blanket and disappear.

"Take it! Quick!"

"All right! Oops! Now see what you made me do! My thumb was on the lens. I got a picture of my thumb. Now we've got to start all over again."

"Hurry!"

But it was too late. Billy Wentworth, in his camouflage T-shirt, peered over the hedge. His monkey eyes landed on Bingo.

He gave a small smile, as if he had come across an enemy without any means of defense. "Here's Misty and her stuff," he said.

"In a minute," Bingo said stiffly. The main reason he had chosen the back of the house was because there was less likelihood of being spotted. Now this!

Wentworth's smile continued. "What are you taking the Worm Brain's picture for?"

"I'm doing it for a friend of mine, you know, Melissa? She wants a picture of him."

"What for?"

"I don't know. What does anybody want a picture for? To look at. Smile, Bingo."

Bingo pulled his lips back into a smile.

"Not like that. Smile like you mean it."

Bingo suddenly remembered how natural it had been to smile at Melissa. Sometimes, at night in the darkness, he had smiled just thinking of smiling at her.

"Perfect!" Cici said. "She'll love it!"

The camera clicked and Bingo started gratefully for the hedge. Without meeting Wentworth's eyes, he took Misty and her suitcase.

Cici followed. She said, "Oh, let me get one of you with the dog. This will be so precious. Hold the dog up! Oh, its face is so sweet. Could I pat it?"

Wentworth said, "Be my guest."

Cici rushed forward and scratched Misty's head with what Bingo now realized were Lee Press-on Nails, some of which needed repressing.

"Oh, and it has a little suitcase for its things. Can I look in it?"

Bingo surrendered the handle of the suitcase and stood stiffly, looking over the roof of his garage.

Cici knelt and unzipped the bag—another awkward move with the Lee Press-ons. She reached inside and pulled out a squeaky rubber newspaper.

"Oh, isn't that precious? It has its own newspaper. And I can tell that it really plays with it. And dog food—oh, it eats Mighty Dog! Why, it's too little for Mighty Dog, or maybe that's why it's eating it." She looked into Misty's damp eyes. "Are you trying to become mighty?"

Yes, Bingo thought, big blonds do not always have brains to match.

Cici browsed through the rest of the suitcase. "Oh, vitamins and a chew stick, and what's this in the bottom?"

"Her blanket," Billy Wentworth said.

Bingo turned in astonishment. He stared at Billy Wentworth. Billy's voice had actually deepened on those two words, "her blanket."

What was happening here?

"It's like a real baby blanket."

"It is a real baby blanket," Wentworth said. His voice was almost purring with pleasure now, like a well-tuned engine. "It was mine."

Bingo's mouth dropped open as he gaped at the faded blue square. Billy Wentworth had once been a baby!

"She doesn't have, like, you know, a basket or bed or something?"

"No, she just drags her blanket around and sleeps where she wants to."

"That's what a little neighbor of mine does! I baby-sit her. Bingo, is this darling little dog yours or"—she nodded to the face above the hedge—"his?"

"His."

"And I," the deep voice from the hedge said, "am Willy Bentworth."

Chicken Chests

Bingo said, "Well, I'll be going now."

He held out his hand for Misty. "The dog, please." He said this in the formal way someone on TV asks for the official envelope.

Cici hugged Misty to her. "I'll carry her inside for you."

"That will not be necessary," Bingo said.

"I can't give her up yet. Please! I just love this little animal." Billy Wentworth cleared his throat in a menacing enemy-sighted way. Bingo shrugged helplessly.

With a flick of her blond hair, a flash of Lee Press-on Nails, Cici turned. Bingo followed her to the steps and went up reluctantly.

In the kitchen Cici spun around and said, "Who was that nerd?"

"Billy Wentworth. You don't know Billy Wentworth?" Then Bingo remembered the deep-throated voice describing the dog blanket and added kindly, "He makes a bad first impression, but you get used to him."

"Ugh, I can't stand jocks."

"Actually, he's not a jock. He's more into army stuff, ammo. He led our T-shirt rebellion last year. Perhaps you saw him standing on the garbage can at recess, or on the school steps, waiting for a face-off with the principal."

"I must have been sick that day. Anyway, I know a jock when I see one. My mom married three of them."

Bingo stood awkwardly in the center of the kitchen. He waited; then, when it became obvious that Cici was not going to leave, he reached manfully for his apron and tied it on.

"You will have to excuse me now, I am preparing, er, chicken chests."

He grimaced. He was sorry he hadn't been cool enough to say breasts, but it was done now.

"Oh, can I watch? I'll sit over here and hold Misty. I won't bother you at all."

"I'd rather you didn't."

"Misty's mouth is already watering for some chicken, isn't it, Misty? Do you have any paper napkins, Bingo?"

Bingo didn't answer. He turned on the oven—350—and bent over his recipe book. He had decided to pretend that no blonds were present.

Misty was watching him with her blank, all-seeing stare, but Bingo ignored that, too.

"Oh, here they are." Cici pulled out a napkin and dabbed at Misty's receding chin. Then she turned her attention to Bingo. "You're probably wondering about how I came to have three jocks for fathers. Everybody does."

She waited for Bingo to answer, but there was only the sound of chicken skin being ripped firmly from chicken breasts.

"The first was my real father. He was a golf pro. He and my mom split up, and she married a man who used to play tight end for the Atlanta Falcons."

Bingo browned the chicken chests. Over the sizzle, he heard, "I was flower girl in that wedding. Then they split up, you know, and my mom married a man who manages the Nautilus. They pump iron together. I was the junior bridesmaid in that wedding."

Bingo poured the sauce over the chicken and slid the casserole into the oven.

"If she ever gets married again, I guess I'll be maid of honor."

Bingo wiped his hands on his apron.

"So, you see, I do know something about jocks."

Bingo got out the salad. He had already cut up the lettuce and vegetables and had planned to toss it, cheflike, at the table as a diversion for his parents. Now he had to do it as a diversion for himself.

"Can I tell you something?"

Bingo said, "If you like," but he did not let up on his tossing.

"You are a wonderful cook," Cici said.

Lettuce fluttered nervously into the air and onto the counter as Bingo's head snapped up in alarm. "No, I'm not. I promise I'm not!"

He was only beginning to understand how important it was that this girl not like him. The thought surprised him.

It had never even occurred to Bingo that the day would come when he would actually want to be disliked.

And, furthermore, he didn't want *any* big blonds to like him. He wanted them to avoid him, to cross the street when they saw him coming.

It was strange how just one experience with a big blond could made a man yearn for a small brunette.

"I'm very careless; I don't measure stuff," he blurted out, gathering up the stray salad and dropping it back in the bowl. "Half the time I don't even wash my hands."

"Real chefs don't either. I've watched them on TV. I wish you could see the way my mom fixes meals. She just, you know, covers everything with bean sprouts."

"Smells good!" Bingo's mom called cheerfully from the front door.

Bingo swirled, stricken.

"Quick! Go out the back door. Give me the dog! Go on! Go!"

"Why?"

"It's my mom!"

"What does your mom have to do with it?"

"Just go!"

Bingo and Cici had a brief tug of war over Misty. Bingo won, but he staggered back and landed hard against the refrigerator door.

Condiment bottles clinked inside. Liquids sloshed. Ice cubes rattled.

"What on earth is going on back there?"

Bingo's mom started across the living room.

"Nothing, Mom," Bingo called. "Don't come in.

Please! I want supper to be a surpr—"

He didn't get to finish because his mom was already there. She stopped in the doorway, taking in the domestic scene. Her eyes narrowed at the sight of the blond.

Bingo put Misty on the floor. He smoothed down his apron modestly.

His mom's face tightened in a way Bingo had never cared for. "So! What is going on back here?"

"She was just leaving," Bingo stammered. "She was holding the dog so I could cook, and then I was trying to get the dog, and she was, well, she was just getting ready to leave, weren't you?"

"Mrs. Brown?" Cici said in a cool, woman-to-woman way.

His mom responded with equal coolness. "Yes?"

"My name is Cici, with two *i*'s, you know, and I probably ought to explain to you why I'm standing here in your kitchen."

"Probably."

Bingo said, "Just go home, please," to Cici.

He turned to his mother with bright desperation. "Mom, I made chicken in tarragon sauce, well, actually it's oregano sauce because we didn't have any tarragon, but since we didn't have the tarragon, I won't count this as one of my meals. I'll just throw it in for—"

His mom said, "Be quiet, Bingo. That can wait. Go on, Cici. I really would like to know what you're doing in my kitchen, if it's not too much trouble."

"It's no trouble at all, Mrs. Brown. You're probably going to think this is silly, but I have this real good friend named Melissa. She moved to Bixby, Oklahoma, last spring. Did you know that?"

"It's come to my attention."

Bingo's mom had gotten new clothes for her real estate career, and when she had them on, she acted—Bingo thought—very, very businesslike, too businesslike.

"Well, Melissa wrote and asked me to take a picture of Bingo, and so I came over with my camera, and after I took his picture—actually, I took two pictures—no, three, but one was of my thumb."

She held up her thumb as if she were bumming a ride. "You know how sometimes you put your thumb on the lens when you're nervous?" She flexed her thumb twice. "I wouldn't have been so nervous if it hadn't been for this nerd looking over the fence. So then . . ."

Bingo closed his eyes as the miserable tale droned on. He leaned back and let the refrigerator keep him from falling to the floor.

Mentally he began going over the multiple listings he would put under "Trials of Today," starting with:

1. A mixed-sex photography session.

Under "Triumphs" he would once again have only the one word: none.

"Cici." Wentworth spoke it like an agreeable Spaniard. Then he said, "How come I never saw her before?"

"She's not in our grade."

"She's older?"

Bingo shook his head.

"Younger?"

Bingo nodded.

"She can't be younger. She's built like a twin-engine—"

"Good night."

Bingo didn't wait to hear what twin-engine vehicle Cici was built like. He collapsed on his bed.

"Knock, knock," his mom said. "Can I come in?"

"Apparently you already are," Bingo said coolly.

"Oh, Bingo, maybe I did misinterpret the scene in the kitchen this afternoon, but when I came in the front door I heard scuffling sounds in the kitchen, and then when I came into the kitchen, there you were with this—this woman!"

Bingo maintained a dignified silence.

"You were against the refrigerator, gasping for breath. Your face was red as a beet. Bingo, you did look guilty. And she was against the sink, also out of breath, also looking guilty. What was I supposed to think?"

Bingo shrugged. "Nothing . . . anything."

For the first time in his life, Bingo was grateful for pronouns. Words that were used as substitutes were especially handy when you didn't know exactly what words they were substituting for.

"Let's just forget it."

Bingo came up with, "Whatever." It was a mark of how

The Pronoun Explosion

Bingo lay on his Smurf sheets. Misty lay on her blanket beside Bingo's bed. Misty was snoring softly. Bingo was awake.

There was a knock at the window.

"I'm not here," Bingo called.

"It's me, Worm Brain."

"I know."

"And it's important."

"Wentworth . . ." It was a plea.

The knocks got louder. Slowly Bingo pulled himself up and went to the window.

Wentworth said, "Hey, you know that blond girl that was taking your picture this afternoon, the one who sort of liked me?"

"Yes."

"What was her name?"

"Cici."

low his life had sunk, that the only thing he had to be grateful for were pronouns.

"Thanks. Oh, Bingo, did I tell you I think I sold the Maynard's house?" She left without waiting for an answer.

Almost immediately there was another knock at the window. Before Bingo could answer it, there was a knock at the door. Bingo swung around helplessly.

His dad stuck his head in Bingo's room. "You got a minute?"

"Sure."

"I just wanted to say that I—"

Knock, knock.

"Excuse me, Dad, I've got to answer the window."

"The window? People knock on your window?"

"Just one." Bingo crossed the room. Wentworth's nose was pressed against the screen.

"What do you want, Wentworth?"

"I'm going on vacation in the morning," Billy said.

Bingo sighed. "I know that," he said with what he thought was great patience. I'm keeping your dog."

"Well, if that girl—the blond one that likes me—Cici? If she asks where I am—"

"Yes?"

"Tell her I'm on vacation."

"I will, Billy. Good night and good-bye."

Bingo came back to the bed. His dad was reclining against the Smurf pillows, his arms behind his head.

"Does he do that often, Bingo?"

"Often enough."

Bingo sat on the edge of the bed. "If it's about this afternoon . . ."

"Your mom may have overreacted on that, Bingo."

"May have? She thought this girl and I were—I don't know exactly what she did think we were doing." Bingo was genuinely offended. "Anyway I would never do stuff like that in a kitchen!"

"Look, Bingo, your mom has always worried that you'd be, well, sort of shy with girls."

"Why would she think that? Were you?"

"No, just the opposite."

"Then why should I be?"

"I don't know. It's what she thought. Then all of a sudden, in the course of a week, she gets a fifty-dollar phone bill from your calls to one girl and then she catches you in the kitchen with another."

"So now she's started worrying that I'm not shy enough."

His dad smiled. "Something like that."

"I didn't even like that girl this afternoon. She's not my type. But when I do like a girl, well, I really, really like her, Dad. I can't help it."

"I couldn't either." His dad looked up at the ceiling. "Over the years there've been, let's see, at least ten girls that I loved like that."

Bingo looked down at his hands in embarrassment. He wished his father would keep personal stuff like that personal.

"The first was JoBeth Ames in kindergarten. I actually married her."

"Dad!"

"Yes, her older sister performed the ceremony. In second grade it was Lisbeth; it was Monica in third; Hazelann in Junior High. Hazelann had a pink angora sweater that used to reach out when I got close to her. Like, I'd pass her in the hall, and this angora stuff would come at me, like I was a magnet. It wouldn't do that for anybody else."

Bingo's dad continued with his eyes closed. "I suppose it was something electrical between us, because the first time we dated, she got in the car and she had on the pink angora sweater and she slid across the seat—we sat close back then—and her hand touched mine, and a big blue spark flashed in the air."

Bingo waited as respectfully as he could, under the circumstances, for his father's eyes to open.

Finally they did and, to Bingo's relief, his dad sat up. "It still happens to me every now and then, and I'm thirty-eight."

"What still happens? Blue sparks?"

His father shook his head.

Bingo tried not to show his alarm. "You fall in love?"

"Well, I don't guess you'd call it love, Bingo. Like last Saturday I went in Eckerd's, and this woman was standing there spraying some sample perfume on the insides of her wrists. Then she touched her wrists together and lifted them to her face, and I fell in love right there in Cosmetics. Now don't get me wrong, Bingo, I have never even thought about being unfaithful to your mom."

"I should hope not."

"Then from Eckerd's I went to Bi-Lo, and a woman in

Produce asked me to help her pick out a good cantaloupe, and as we were—"

"You fell in love in Bi-Lo, too?"

Now Bingo's voice was high with alarm. It was bad enough to hear of old loves, old wedding ceremonies, old blue sparks. Hearing of new stuff made Bingo want to put his fingers in his ears.

His father broke off and said briskly, "Well, I've gotten off the subject. I didn't come in to talk about my weaknesses."

Bingo took a deep breath to calm himself. He had always known his parents were blind to the depths of his own feelings. They had proved that again and again. But apparently he had been somewhat blind, too.

As soon as he could speak normally, he said, "So what do you want to talk about?"

"Well, just that despite the incident of the phone bill, Bingo, your mom and I have been very pleased with you this summer."

"You have?" Bingo felt they had managed to hide their pleasure rather successfully.

"I myself have had the feeling that the three of us, well, this summer it's been more like three adults living in the same house. It's been actually peaceful. Then, when you started fixing supper, well, your mom was so happy. It was a thrill for her to come home to a good supper."

"I don't know about good," Bingo said. "She scraped every bit of oregano sauce off her chicken."

"She was upset."

"Well, I was, too, but I ate mine. Dad, I prepared that sauce under very difficult circumstances with a girl—only she's more like a college girl, Dad—following me around. I need privacy to cook. I'm not the Galloping Gourmet."

"Your mom's under a strain right now."

"What kind of strain?" Bingo paused. Had he been blind to his mother's feelings, too? "I thought Mom loved her job. She never talks about anything else."

"She does love her job. If anything she loves it too much."

"She's not going to get fired, is she?"

"No, but . . ." His dad got up quickly. "Look, I better let you get some sleep. Good night, Bingo."

"I'd like to know what kind of strain," Bingo began. "Wait a minute."

But his father was closing the door behind him. Suddenly Bingo was very tired. It had been a long, hard day. He would find out about his mother's strain tomorrow.

"Good night, Dad."

Bingo lay down on the Smurf sheets and closed his eyes. As he tried to sleep, burning questions trotted across his mind instead of sheep.

When I am a father, will I fall in love in Eckerd's and Bi-Lo?

Can a gene for this kind of masculine weakness be passed on from father to son?

Aren't there some indications that the unfortunate gene has, indeed, been passed on?

When I am thirty-eight, if someone asks me to help them

pick a good cantaloupe, will I be able to do this without blushing or—worse! *Worse!* Will I actually hang out at the cantaloupe counter, hoping someone will ask?

Finally, at last, Bingo slept.

The Missing Vital Organ

Bingo had a strange, empty feeling.

It wasn't hunger. He ate and he still had it. It wasn't thirst. He drank a lot of pop, too. Bingo didn't know exactly what it was. It was just a huge internal void.

It was as if some vital organ had been secretly removed from his body and beamed up to some alien. And now this alien was stretched out contentedly, saying, "Ah," while on earth Bingo suffered in confusion.

Perhaps, Bingo thought, he could use this empty feeling later in one of his science-fiction novels, but now he could only wait for it to pass.

This was the third day of the emptiness. It had started that terrible afternoon when his mother had mistaken the incident in the kitchen for a romantic encounter. Ever since then, there had been this emptiness, which was not improving. If anything, he was getting more empty.

Bingo got up from the sofa. He said, "Come on, Misty. Let's go to the store."

At the sight of her leash, Misty began trembling with excitement.

"Don't get your hopes up. I'm just going for some noodles and a can of tuna. Tonight I'm making tuna lasagna."

Bingo hooked the leash on Misty's rhinestone collar. He was glad to have Misty these days. With this terrible three-day emptiness, he needed both companionship and eye contact. Misty's eyes watered a lot, so it was especially satisfying to tell her his troubles.

He and Misty were going down the steps when the mailman arrived. "I'll take those," Bingo said. He glanced down and stopped in place.

The top letter had his name on it. Mr. Bingo Brown. He loved the way his name looked with a *Mr.* in front of it. A name like Bingo needed a *Mr.*

He lifted the envelope and held it in his hand, as if weighing it. He smelled it for the scent of gingersnaps, but the letter only smelled like U. S. mail.

Bingo wondered if he would be able to control himself when Melissa started using perfume. If the scent of gingersnaps sometimes drove him mad, what would perfume—which was a chemical actually designed to drive men mad—do to him? Could he—

Misty whined at the end of her leash.

"In a minute, Misty."

He put the rest of the mail in the box and, slipping the end of the leash on his wrist like a bracelet, he opened his letter.

Dear Bingo,

I was really glad to get your letter, because after your phone calls stopped, I thought you had forgotten I was alive.

I've seen my new school, but I know I'm not going to like it as much as Roosevelt Middle School. For one thing, you won't be there.

A girl in my apartment building says the science teacher is neat. As you know, I'm going to be a scientist and a rock star, so this is important to me.

Bingo stopped for a moment, remembering the day Melissa had announced her dual careers to the class. "I am going to be a scientist and a rock star." It had been like a movie he had seen recently, and he had fallen instantly in love with Dr. Jekyll and Ms. Hyde.

He went back to the letter.

I wrote Mr. Mark a letter, giving him my new address, but he hasn't written back yet.

I think of you a lot, Bingo. I hope sometime I'll get back to see you, or maybe you could come out to Bixby for a visit. You ask your mom and I'll ask mine.

                        Love forever,
                        Melissa

P. S. I asked my best friend, Cici, to come over and take a picture of you. You probably don't know Cici, but she knows you because I

pointed you out to her in the hall one day. If
you don't want to have the picture taken, you
don't have to.

Bingo stopped at the corner. While waiting for traffic,
he put the letter in his pocket. Then he picked up Misty
so they could cross the street. He had already learned that
Misty was so afraid of cars she tried to run under them
for safety. Above all, he did not want to have to say to
Billy Wentworth, "Remember that dog I was keeping for
you? Well, she got run over."

He put Misty down on the sidewalk, and they continued
walking.

Bingo said, "Misty, I could never go to Bixby. For one
thing, my mom wouldn't let me. And also, Misty, I don't
particularly want to go.

"Oh, I wouldn't mind going somewhere. I like to travel.
A plane ride, even a train or bus trip would probably do
me a lot of good right now."

He paused before he went on. "What I wouldn't like would be getting there . . . being there . . ."

He stumbled and gasped. Misty came to the end of her leash and looked around, her wet eyes startled.

"Oh, Misty," he said.

He clasped his free hand over his heart.

Now Bingo realized what had happened to him. He realized what the terrible, empty void was.

He looked up at the sky as if the answer had come directly from there.

Of course he was empty!

He had every right to feel empty!

He would be an inhuman beast if he didn't feel empty!

"Misty," Bingo said with infinite sadness. "I am no longer in love."

Misty was looking back at him, holding eye contact. Her tail trembled.

"I don't know how it happened. How could a person be in love for eternity, no, for infinity, and then"—he shrugged helplessly—"then, *nothing!*"

Misty waited.

"This is the first time in six, no, seven months that I've been without a real burning desire, and I don't use that word 'burning' lightly. No wonder I've been feeling terrible. I'm the kind of person who has to have a burning desire."

He picked Misty up and tucked her under his arm for comfort.

"Perhaps I won't have any trouble falling in love again. After all, one time I fell in love with three girls in ten minutes, and my dad still falls in love at drug stores and supermarkets. I got the gene from him.

"But, Misty, would anybody other than Melissa fall in love with me? Having Melissa fall in love with me was pretty much a miracle, to be honest with you, and how many miracles happen to a person in one lifetime?"

The Bi-Lo doors parted, and Bingo entered the store. He walked purposefully through Produce, Dairy Products, and Cold Cuts.

"I must do one thing before I get the noodles. I want to go to the cookie aisle and smell the gingersnaps. This is a test, Misty. Because if I don't feel like calling Melissa when I smell gingersnaps, then I'll know for sure. See, the first time I rode in a car with Melissa—our substitute teacher was taking us to the hospital to visit Mr. Mark—as we got in the car, Melissa brushed against me, and I smelled gingersnaps. Ever since then . . ."

Bingo trailed off and reached for the gingersnap box. He took it down and stood looking at the picture of the round, cheerful, brown cookies.

An expression of sorrow came over Bingo's face. He returned the box gently to the shelf.

"Yes," he told Misty, "it's over."

As Bingo got his groceries and headed for the check-out counter, he thought how life had a way of U-turning.

At one time in his life he had wanted desperately to fall out of love with Melissa. He had been in love with Melissa and Harriet and Mamie Lou at the time, and he would have given anything, anything to fall out of love with any of them; he didn't even care which.

Without thinking about it twice, he would have put under

"Triumphs of Today":

1. Falling out of love with Melissa.

But times had changed; life had made one of its cruel U-turns. Now he would put it firmly under "Trials."

Double Phone Calls

"The wonderful smell you smell," Bingo called, "is tuna lasagna."

Bingo opened the oven door so his mom could get the full effect.

He waited with his hands in his apron pockets, smiling, for his mom to put her head in the door and compliment him. Actually his mom seemed to like the smell of his food better than the food itself, but tonight would be different. Tonight he had followed the recipe exactly.

At last he had something solid to put in his summer journal. Indeed, he was so sure of himself he had already envisioned it in his notebook. "Triumphs of Today":

1. Tuna lasagna!!!!!

Later he might add his parents' admiring comments: "Delicious, Bingo. . . . Outstanding, Son."

At one time he might have considered tuna lasagna too

insignificant to list, but with the way his life was going, any and all triumphs, including just getting through the day, counted.

Bingo continued to wait.

Instead of poking her head in the kitchen, his mother went through the living room, directly to her bedroom.

Bingo heard the door shut.

"Mom?"

He went out into the hall.

"Mom?" There was a long silence, so Bingo filled it with another, "Mom?"

"Bingo, I'm lying down."

"Is it something I've done?"

"No."

"Is it something I haven't done?"

"No."

"Is it—"

"Bingo, let me alone."

Bingo went slowly back to the kitchen. He was standing by the stove, idly tapping the front burner, wondering what to do next, when the phone rang.

"Get that, Bingo," his mother called.

"All right."

"I don't want to talk to anybody unless it's Mom."

"How about Dad?"

"No!"

Bingo hesitated. Then he picked up the phone. "Hello."

"Bingo, hi. It's Cici. I'm sooo glad you answered, because I know your mom doesn't like me. I can always tell when people don't like me, because their eyes seem to shoot little darts, you know? Even your mom's voice shoots—"

"Why are you calling?" Bingo interrupted formally.

"Oh, I got the pictures back. Bingo, they are so good. They look professional. I'm even thinking about becoming a professional photographer. And they all three came out, even the one when my thumb was over the lens!"

"That's nice."

"I'm going to send one to Melissa and one to you, and I'm going to keep one for myself—the one of you with the poodle. That's my favorite. But, Bingo, I want you to see them all before I—"

"That won't be necessary."

"I want you to. I could come over right now. I never have enough to do in the summer, Bingo. That's why I was sooo glad when Melissa asked me to take your picture."

"Don't come over!"

"Bingo, are you mad at me?"

"No. I just don't want you to come over."

"I knew it! You *are* mad!"

"No, no, I'm not mad. I can't have girls over anymore. It's a rule."

"Is your mom there?"

"Yes."

"Well, we could meet somewhere—the park. Oh, I know! The miniature golf course! We could, like, play golf! Your mom couldn't get mad if we played miniature golf, could she?"

At that unfortunate moment, Bingo's mom picked up the phone in her bedroom.

She said coldly, "Bingo, I want to use the phone now."

"I was just hanging up."

Bingo put the phone down without saying good-bye. Then he walked softly through the house. He stopped at the door of his mother's room.

Bingo didn't intend to listen, but the scent of something wrong drew him as surely as the scent of gingersnaps had once drawn him to the phone. He stood with his apron anxiously bunched up at his waist.

His mom had finished dialing. She waited silently. Bingo did, too.

At last she spoke. "Mom, hi. It's me. . . . Yes, I just got back. . . . Yes . . . Yes . . . Mom, I don't know what I'm going to do. . . ."

Bingo's mom's voice seemed to break on the words, as if she were crying. Bingo had never seen either one of his parents cry. In his alarm, he stepped closer to the door and pressed his ear against it.

His mom said, "You wouldn't mind? You aren't busy? I thought this was your evening for CUT! I don't want you to miss—"

This really alarmed Bingo. He closed his eyes and tried to breathe normally.

Bingo's grandmother was a charter member of CUT!— Clean Up Townsville! And this weekend she was leading a protest at a convenience store where *Penthouse* and *Playboy* were being sold.

If the protest was Saturday, then tonight would be the rally! Only the most serious situation would cause his grandmother to miss the rally!

His mother said gratefully, "Oh, Mom, thank you. I'll be right over."

There was a pause. Bingo stepped back from the door, but his mom did not come out. She crossed the room and whipped paper from the typewriter. The paper tore.

Bingo drew in a breath of deep alarm.

His father's story! His mom had torn the short story his father was writing out of the typewriter. Only the bitterest hatred could cause her to destroy his manuscript. She knew how hard he—

But, no, now she was putting paper back into the typewriter, rolling it into place. She began to type.

There was, of course, no way to tell what she was typing by eavesdropping, but Bingo bent closer to the door anyway.

Then his mother came out of the door so fast she almost knocked Bingo down. "Are you going to Grammy's?" Bingo gasped.

"Yes."

"Can I come?"

"No." The sheet of paper was in her hand. Bingo caught the first three words as she folded it. "I have gone . . ."

"Why?"

"Not this time."

"But why?"

Bingo followed his mom into the living room. She paused to stick the note under the edge of the VCR. This was where they left messages for each other. Then she went onto the porch. Bingo went down the steps behind her.

"Why can't I come?"

His mom got to the curb before him. She had parked her car with the wheels turned into the curb, so when she started off, she drove up on the curb as if she were aiming directly at Bingo.

He jumped back. "Mom!"

She was busy bumping the car back onto the street. This increased Bingo's alarm. Usually his mom was a careful driver.

"Mom?" He ran after her. "Mom!"

"What?"

She braked then and looked at him out of the back window. Her face was as puzzled as if she was trying to figure out who he was.

"Will you be back for supper?"

"No."

"Mom, it's tuna lasagna."

"I'm not hungry."

Then, with Bingo staring after her, she drove away. Bingo watched until she drove around the corner, tires squealing, and disappeared from sight.

Bingo went quickly back into the house. He stopped at the VCR and stood looking at the folded sheet of paper under it.

The Loving Wofe

Bingo lifted the edge of the paper and read.

"I have gone to Mom's! Do not follow me. Do not call. I mean it, Sam. I need time. I need space. I do not need you badgering me. Keep away!"

Bingo drew in a deep breath. The short, hurtful sentences hit his heart like a hammer.

And if these eight sentences hurt him, what would they do to his father? They were *to* his father. He could not bear for his father to stand here and—

Perhaps if he added something . . . "With love." Yes, a "With Love" would definitely take away some of the sting.

Bingo took the note into his parents' room and rolled it into the typewriter. At the bottom of his mother's short sentences he typed, "Your loving wife." That was even better than "With love." He pulled out the sheet. He gasped. He had typed, "Your loving wofe."

He was reaching for the eraser when he heard his father coming up the front steps.

He raced into the living room, stuck the note back under the VCR, and ran for the kitchen. He turned on the water and stood with his eyes closed, heart thumping, lungs struggling. He imagined his father coming into the living room, checking under the VCR, reading the note.

He groaned, remembering the *wofe*. Perhaps he could say, "Mom must have been terribly upset. Look at the way she spelled wife." Or, "What's a wofe, Dad? I don't believe I ever heard of a—"

His dad came into the kitchen. "Where's your mom?" he asked.

Bingo's eyes snapped open. "I don't know. She went out." It was a childish recitation. "She might have left a note. Did you check under the VCR?"

"No."

"There's a piece of paper there. It could be a note."

"What does the note say, Bingo?"

"How should I—"

"You're the resident specialist on notes," his father said with unusual tenseness. "What does it say?"

"I don't remember the exact words."

Bingo knew the eight sentences by heart, but it would be painful enough to read them in private. To hear one's son recite them would be unbearable.

Bingo's father went into the living room. Bingo waited in the kitchen.

His father came back, note in hand.

"What time did your mom leave?"

"About a half hour ago."

"What did she say?"

"Not much. Just that she was going to Grammy's and I couldn't go with her. Then I asked if she would be home for supper, and she said she wasn't hungry. Then she drove off, and, Dad, she came up onto the curb. Right at me! Dad, I had to jump out of the way to keep from getting hit. What's wrong? What's going on?"

His dad ran his hands through his hair. "Let me try calling her."

"Dad, she said not to call. The note said, 'Do not follow me. Do not call.' "

His father went to the phone, and Bingo followed like a toy on a string. Bingo waited in silence while his father dialed. The phone rang four times, and then his grandmother's recorded message came on. "This is Rosemary Harrison. I can't receive your call, but if you'd like to leave a message, I'll get back to you. And remember, support CUT! Let's clean up Townsville!"

At the beep, Bingo's dad said, "Nance, I know you're there. I know you can hear me. Pick up the phone. Now!"

In a small voice, Bingo said, "The note also said, 'Do not badger me.' "

"They are the only two women in the world who can sit there while someone is begging to talk to them." His father said tensely into the receiver, "Nance, answer the phone."

Bingo cleared his throat. "Maybe they went out."

His dad shook his head. "They're there. I know they are. They're sitting side by side on the sofa. Either one of them could reach the phone if they wanted to."

"They could have gone—" Bingo began, but a look from his father caused him to trail off.

"Every time something happens, Nance runs to her mother. Other women turn to their husbands. She turns to her mother."

He hung up the phone so hard it gave a ring of its own in protest.

"Well, I'm not going to sit around here, waiting," his dad said. "I'm going over there. Maybe they'll answer the door. If not, I'll break the damn thing down."

Bingo said quickly, "I'll go with you."

"No, you stay here. If she does come home, somebody ought to be here."

"Dad, you'll need help with the door. I can—"

"Please, Bingo."

Bingo trailed his father onto the porch. "But what did you mean when you said 'every time something happens.' What has happened? I don't know what's going on!"

Shaking his head as if it was too much for him, Bingo's dad got in the car. Bingo stood for a moment, watching him drive away. Then he went back and sat down on the steps.

There was a whine at the door. Bingo glanced over his shoulder.

"Oh, sorry, Misty. I didn't mean to leave you. I know how it feels to be left, believe me."

He opened the screen door, and Misty came out. Her toenails clicked softly against the floorboards.

Bingo patted the board beside him, and Misty sat. Bingo

stared at the late afternoon sun. Misty stared at Bingo. Idly, Bingo rubbed the dog's head.

"Misty, I now have the most important question that I've ever had in my whole life—and I have had a lot of questions. I once filled an entire notebook full, *full* of questions, Misty. I didn't skip a single line."

Perhaps it was Bingo's urgent need to have someone to communicate with, but it did seem to him that Misty actually nodded her head. At any rate, her eyes were watering sympathetically. Misty listened almost as tenderly as Melissa.

"But, Misty, this is the kind of question that I know, I *know* I don't want the answer to. Because whatever is happening with my parents is something that I don't want to hear. When you have a question and it's the kind of question that you know you won't be able to bear the answer, well, that is the worst kind of question there is. It's like a terrible burden. Your body feels like it's actually being weighted down by—"

"Hi."

Bingo gasped.

"Did I scare you?"

A big blond was the last person a man wanted to see in moments of anxiety, and that's what this was—Cici.

Bingo followed his gasp with a silence.

"I saw that you were talking to Misty, and I didn't want to interrupt, but I had to because, Bingo, I had to! Bingo, I may have done a really, truly terrible thing."

Tears filled Cici's eyes. Bingo's hands began to twitch with unrealized gestures. Why did his hands do this every

time he talked to a girl? He wished he had normal, con-
trollable hands like everybody else.

He stuffed his hands into his pockets. "Oh?"

"Bingo?"

"Yes."

More tears. Any minute they would spill over. Bingo
straightened anxiously. A big blond's tears could be as
disturbing as anybody else's if they spilled.

"Bingo?"

"Yes?"

"Bingo . . ."

"What? You must tell me!"

"Well, I was sending you one of the pictures and Melissa
one of the pictures, and I wrote each of you a letter to go
with the picture. But when I got ready to mail them, my
mom was making me hurry because I was getting a body
wave, and, Bingo . . ."

"Yes!"

"Oh, Bingo . . ."

Bingo waited. He clasped one hand around his throat
to keep his heart from moving up into his head.

"Bingo, I think I sent Melissa's letter to you and yours
to Melissa."

Bingo's shoulders collapsed with relief. "Oh, is that all?
That's nothing, nothing," he said gallantly.

"You don't know what the letters said."

"Well, that's true, but—"

"If you did, you wouldn't say it was nothing."

"Oh?"

"You would say it was, like, the opposite of nothing."

Bingo waited. He was incapable of further speech. He had even used up all his *oh*s.

"So, Bingo, I have come to ask for a favor."

Bingo waited limply.

"When you get your letter and open it, if you see that it starts out 'Dear Melissa,' please don't read the rest, please! Promise!"

"I never read other people's mail."

"You mean that?"

Bingo nodded.

"Oh, Bingo, you are just as nice as Melissa always said you were. Thank you, thank—"

For one terrible moment Bingo thought she was going to take his hand. Maybe even press her lips against it.

He got quickly to his feet. He folded his arms around Misty and tucked his hands in his armpits.

Anyway, he knew one thing. He had had enough mixed-sex conversations to last him an eternity, even infinity. The *National Enquirer* could do what they would with it. "Boy Swears Off Mixed-Sex Conversations for Infinity."

"I have to go now," he said.

"Did I come at a bad time? I'm sorry. But I just saw you sitting there, you know, and I had to stop you from reading the letter. I just had to. You just don't know what the letter said or you'd—"

Bingo reached for the doorknob.

"Excuse me. I have something important to do."

"Cook?"

Bingo shook his head and went into the house.

He had not lied. He did have something important to

do, one of the most important things he had ever done in
his life: collapse.

He did this on the sofa, with Misty in the crook of his
arm like a football.

The scent of overcooked lasagna flowed from the
kitchen, calling him, but Bingo did not respond.

The Kiss

Bingo lay with his eyes closed. He was trying to remember the last time his mom and dad had been happy, the last time he had seen them happy.

He sighed as he remembered. The last time his mom and dad had been happy was the worst day of Bingo's life—the rainy afternoon he and Melissa had said good-bye.

It was the day Melissa had moved. The rain had been falling steadily since dawn.

Bingo had intended to ride his bike over to say good-bye, but because it was raining so hard, his parents drove him. After Bingo's good-bye, they were going to Bingo's grandmother's birthday supper.

The car was full of presents and balloons, and the balloons were for some reason attracted to Bingo's dad. They kept bobbing over to his head.

His dad batted them away. "Nance, get these fool balloons away from me. Why do they keep coming at my head?"

"They probably recognize a similar empty space and think it's one of them." His mom laughed.

"This is not funny, Nance. I'm going to have a wreck if these balloons don't leave me alone."

Bingo had not joined in the laughter. He was going to say good-bye to the woman he loved.

They pulled up in front of Melissa's, and Bingo got out. The front porch was like a stage. The light was on; the curtain seemed to be rising.

Bingo climbed the steps and stood at the door. Movers, Melissa's brothers, her mother passed around him. Bingo was only aware of the door that Melissa would come through.

At last she came. The sight of her made him weak in the knees.

She had on bibbed shorts and a flashy green shirt. There was a pink ribbon in her gypsy hair. She said softly, "Hi, Bingo."

He said, "Hi."

She said, "I was afraid we wouldn't get to say good-bye."

He said, "I wouldn't have let that happen."

There was a pause while they looked at each other. They had eye contact. When you had eye contact with Melissa, Bingo realized, you knew you were having eye contact. He felt as if his eyes were popping out of his head.

Blindly, he groped for her hand. Her fingers curled around his.

Melissa said, "Will you write to me?"

Suddenly, with a start, Bingo realized that what Melissa was really saying was, "Will you love me forever?"

Bingo said, "Yes, I will. Will you answer?" He meant, "Yes, and will you love me back forever?"

She understood! He could see it in her eyes!

She said, "Yes."

Bingo was exhilarated. It was like speaking a foreign language that no one else can understand, so you can speak it freely! Anywhere! Even in front of Melissa's brothers and mother!

They were speaking— Bingo gasped with insight. This was the language of love.

"Bingo!" It was his mother calling from the car. "We've got to go!"

He turned back to Melissa. "Well, good-bye." He meant, "This is *not* good-bye."

"Bye, Bingo." She meant, "Not by a long shot!"

Bingo took a deep, manly breath. The moist air that filled his lungs thrilled him.

He looked down at her. Her face was lit up as if by moonlight. Bingo realized that there was only so much that could be done with words. Even the language of love had its limitations.

Bingo bent then, recklessly, to kiss Melissa's cheek. He wanted to kiss her mouth, of course, but he felt Melissa's mom had her eye on him.

At the very moment he leaned forward, Melissa's mom said, "Oh, Melissa, I want you to—" Melissa turned toward her mom *and* toward Bingo's lips.

Bingo kissed her mouth.

Bingo kissed Melissa's mouth!

He only caught the corner, but—*but*! Just kissing the corner of her mouth had been so thrilling that something under his ribs, something he didn't even know he had— maybe it was his stomach, he couldn't be sure—anyway, this something flipped over.

He knew it had been the same for Melissa because she had her hand over her ribs, too.

He had a tumbling sensation, though he wasn't falling. There was the faint scent of gingersnaps in the damp air.

Honk! Honk!

"Bingo! Come on! We're ready to go!"

He must have walked to the car. He must have gotten in. But it was like watching slides. In one slide he was on the porch staring into Melissa's eyes. Then *click*! He was in the car, watching her through the rain.

As they drove away, Bingo thought that he and Melissa belonged together. They were like two halves of an apple, a matching pair of socks, salt and pepper shakers—

Bingo's father interrupted his thoughts. "Are you asleep, Son?"

Bingo's eyes snapped open. "What time is it?"

"Almost eleven."

Bingo looked around the living room. He blinked. He had been lying on the sofa since Cici left. Misty was still in the crook of his arm, snoring softly.

"Is Mom with you?"

"No."

"Where is she?"

"She's at your grandmother's."

"Still?"

"Yes."

"Is she ever coming home?"

"I hope so." His dad ran his hands through his hair. "Look, I've got to have something to eat, and then we'll talk if you want to."

Bingo said, "Oh, there's lasagna."

He followed his dad into the kitchen and opened the oven door. The lasagna had hardened into a small ill-smelling dark ball. He and his father eyed it together.

"You know what I feel like having?" His dad moved

toward the pantry, hands on his hips, stretching to ease
his back.

"What?"

"Popcorn with milk. Want some?"

"I guess." Bingo didn't meet his father's tired eyes. He
knew that when his dad was a boy, his favorite food had
been popcorn and milk.

It seemed to Bingo that both his parents were going into
reverse. His mom was at her mother's, sleeping in the twin
bed she had slept in as a girl. His dad was eating little kid
food out of a bowl. He alone was continuing to age, and
at an alarming rate.

Bingo sat down at the table. When Bingo's dad put his
bowl of popcorn before him, Bingo ate it slowly, one piece
at a time. He watched his father so intently that sometimes
he raised an empty spoon to his mouth.

His dad finished first and said, "Well." He pushed back
his bowl. "Bingo . . ." He spread his freckled hands flat on
the table.

"Yes?"

"Well, I know you've been aware that . . ."

He trailed off. Bingo said firmly, "I've been aware that
something is very, very wrong," to get the conversation
back on track.

His father said, "Yes, Bingo. This afternoon your mother
found out for sure that—"

There was the sound of a car horn in the driveway. Billy
Wentworth shouted, "Misty, Misty, we're home! We're
back!"

Then Mrs. Wentworth's voice said, "Billy, don't wake the Browns. It's after eleven."

"The lights are on! They're up! I see them! They're still eating! Misty!"

His sister said, "I'll get Misty, Billy. You help Dad with the suitcases."

"She's staying at *my* friend's house," Wentworth said, "so I'll get her."

There was a noisy competition on the front steps. Then Billy knocked loudly on the screen.

"Hey, Bingo! I'm here for *my* dog!"

Misty came out from under the table and looked at Bingo, her wet eyes confused.

"Bad news; they're back," Bingo said. "You got to go home."

As he picked up Misty, he glanced at his father, who was sitting with his head bowed. "I'll be right back," he said.

He carried Misty to the front door, bending as he went to pick up the blanket. "Here," he said, opening the door.

"Misty," Billy's sister cried.

"Get back! She's mine!" Billy said.

Bingo thrust the dog into the tangle of arms, U-turned, and went straight to the kitchen.

His father was waiting as Bingo had left him, freckled hands spread flat on either side of his bowl, head bowed.

Bingo took the seat opposite him. It was, Bingo thought, like people visiting in a prison waiting room, people who'd been apart so long they'd forgotten how to communicate.

His dad cleared his throat. "Bingo," he said.

"Yes, go on."

"Bingo, your mom found out today . . . found out for sure today . . . that . . . Bingo, your mother's pregnant."

Madness at Midnight

Bingo let out a sharp cry of pain, an animal sound he had not known his lungs and vocal cords were capable of.

He closed his eyes. He tried to regulate his breathing, to slow his racing heart, to bring his body back to the normalcy of ten minutes ago.

His dad was saying, "It would have been wonderful if it had happened ten years ago. Your mom wanted a second child then, a little brother or sister for you."

Blindly, Bingo drew in his breath. The thought was so alien, so unthinkable that his brain refused to process it.

It had never even occurred to him ten years ago that his parents might be considering such a reckless act. He had assumed that he would be child enough for any family.

And all the while, as he lay sleeping peacefully in the glow of his Mickey Mouse night light, they had been plotting madness. This was not the correct word, but Bingo was too tired to word search. Madness was good enough.

"But it didn't happen and it didn't happen," his dad continued, "and so your mom accepted that it wouldn't happen and got on with her life."

Bingo's tongue flicked over his dry lips. He was breathing so rapidly through his mouth that his lips were already dry again.

"You know, Bingo, something that would make a person, like your mom, very happy at one point in her life, say when she's twenty-eight, doesn't make her so happy when she's thirty-eight."

Another one of life's cruel twists of fate, Bingo thought. It was as if their lives were being governed by a capricious child. "You want it now? Well, you can't have it." "You don't want it anymore? Well, here it is, pal."

"I guess not."

As he spoke, Bingo opened his eyes and looked at the world. Surprisingly, it was exactly the same.

"When she told me she thought she was going to have a baby—this was last week, before her appointment with the doctor—well, I made the mistake of being happy about it. I was happy about it, Bingo, but I probably shouldn't have shown it so quickly."

"Why not?"

"Certainly not before I showed concern for *her* feelings. Your mom got angry with me. Your mom can get very angry when she wants to, Bingo."

"I know."

"She said, 'Well, of course you'd be happy, it won't affect *you*. It's not *your* job. It's not *your* life.' See, Bingo, after years of lousy jobs—selling Mary Kay cosmetics, Tupperware—she's finally got something interesting, something challenging."

He shook his head. "Then today, when she found out for sure, she called me, and before I could say a word, she yelled, 'Yes, and do you realize that when this baby is Bingo's age, I'll be fifty?' Then she hung up."

Bingo did a little quick arithmetic of his own. When this baby is my age, I'll be— He gasped aloud.

"Anything wrong?" his father asked.

"I'll be twenty-four," Bingo said. He repeated the unhappy number to himself. Twenty-four! He wished he had a phone in his hand so he could slam down the receiver the way his mother had. Twenty-four—Bam!

His father went on as if Bingo had not spoken. "So now she doesn't even want to talk to me about it at all. Actually, we're both too upset to talk sensibly."

"Me too."

"We'll work it out, but right now she's over at your grandmother's—"

"You saw her?"

"Oh, yes. They were sitting on the sofa, right where I knew they'd be, and your grandmother'd been saying all the right things—"

Bingo interrupted. "Like what? What would be the right things?"

"Like, 'I know you're upset; you have every right to be. It will work out. I'll help you. You're a strong person, you always have been.' Things like that, things I should have said. . . ."

"Oh."

At any other time, Bingo might have sympathized with his dad because he himself frequently said the wrong thing. Like right now. If it wasn't for *oh,* Bingo would not have been able to say anything at all. But his sympathies were all for himself.

He remembered a book his dad had had last November during election. His dad had worked at the polls, and they had given him a book titled *What to Do If.* And in this book were listed all the things that could possibly go wrong and what to do about them.

Bingo needed a book like that. And he needed it now. It would give him comfort to turn to the index.

"What to Do If: Your parents let you down by belatedly conceiving a sibling, pp. 41–45."

What relief to turn to page forty-one and—

His dad blew out all the air in his lungs as he got to his feet. He was like a whale coming up after a particularly deep dive.

"Bingo, I've got to go to bed. I've had it."

"I'm tired, too."

"We'll talk tomorrow."

"Yes."

"It's going to work out somehow, Bingo."

Bingo nodded, watching the shriveled pieces of popcorn floating on the milk in his bowl.

His dad paused in the doorway. "Aren't you coming to bed?"

"I'll just clean up. . . ." Bingo made a magicianlike gesture over the table, as if to wave away the hard ball of lasagna, the wet popcorn.

"Well, don't be too late."

"No."

Bingo kept sitting there until he heard the sound of running water in the bathroom. Then he got slowly to his feet.

"Actually, it's already too late," he said.

He was sorry Misty was not there to look at him with her sympathetic, tearful eyes. He wondered if it was too late to go over and borrow Misty. He knew if he told the Wentworths why he needed her, they would hand her over with sympathetic, tearful eyes of their own.

With leaden arms, Bingo began to clear the table.

Purple Smurfs

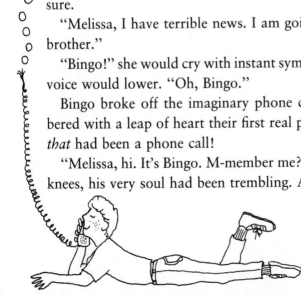

Bingo was having an imaginary phone call with Melissa, since that was the only kind he was allowed to have these days.

"Melissa, hi. It's me, Bingo."

Of course he could not speak the language of love. He was no longer eligible. He would have to get right to the point, before her voice had a chance to deepen with pleasure.

"Melissa, I have terrible news. I am going to become a brother."

"Bingo!" she would cry with instant sympathy. Then her voice would lower. "Oh, Bingo."

Bingo broke off the imaginary phone call. He remembered with a leap of heart their first real phone call. Now *that* had been a phone call!

"Melissa, hi. It's Bingo. M-member me?" His hands, his knees, his very soul had been trembling. Also his voice.

"Bingo, is it really you?"

"Yes."

"This isn't someone playing a joke?"

"No."

"Oh, I was hoping it would be you. When I heard the phone ring, I started hoping. Bingo, guess what?"

"What?"

"This is the first phone call I've gotten since we moved to Bixby."

"Really?"

"Yes, and you know something else?"

"What?"

"If I could only have one phone call, this is the phone call I would want to have."

A rush of burning questions brought Bingo back to the present. Will Melissa still love me when she knows I'm a brother? Can anyone love a person who may be dealing in dirty diapers? Will I be able to deal with diapers without collapsing? Does—

There was a knock at Bingo's window.

Bingo closed his eyes, ignoring it.

"Hey, Worm Brain, it's me."

Bingo did not get up. "What do you want, Wentworth?"

"It's personal."

Still Bingo did not move.

"It's about you-know-who." A pause. "And you better get up off your you-know-what."

Could the news about the baby be out already? Had Billy Wentworth rushed over to be the first to taunt him? Was Wentworth too embarrassed to taunt him? Had he

come to terrorize him? To say, "I don't want to live next
to no big brother?"

Bingo pulled himself slowly up from his Smurf sheets
and crossed the room.

"Get it over with, Wentworth," he said, leaning tiredly
against the window.

Wentworth said, "Listen, you know that girl who was
taking your picture?"

Bingo said, "What?"

"The blond girl. Remember I asked you to tell her that
I was on vacation when she asked where I was?"

"Yes."

"So did you tell her?"

"No."

"Why not?"

"She didn't ask."

"Come on. Quit lying. I know she asked."

"No."

Wentworth hesitated. Bingo glanced over his shoulder
at his bed. He noticed that his mom had not changed his
sheets in so long the Smurfs had turned an ugly purplish
gray. Very few people, Bingo thought, could rest on Smurfs
that unfortunate color, even if their world had not come
crumbling down around them. Still, he wanted to sink
down among them and lay his tired head.

"Let's go over there," Billy Wentworth went on in a
rush.

"Where?"

"To her house, Worm Brain."

"Whose house?"

"*Her* house."

"What for?"

"To tell her I'm back."

"You go. I'm not feeling so hot, Wentworth."

"Look, just ride over there with me. That's all I'm asking. Go up to the door with me. We're pals, aren't we? Just stand there. I'll do all the talking. You won't have to say a word."

"So why do I have to be there?"

"I'll look stupid if I'm by myself. What do you think? You think I want to go around looking stupid, Worm Brain? You can stand there looking stupid for both of us. You got a natural talent for that."

Bingo said, "I'm really not feeling all that good."

"You don't want to feel worse, do you?"

"I'll get my bike."

Bingo and Billy Wentworth pedaled slowly toward Cici's house. Bingo knew the way because Cici lived next door to Melissa's old house. This, Bingo knew, was bound to bring more pain—seeing the very door that she had walked out of, seeing the very front porch where he had kissed her.

It seemed to Bingo, as he pedaled, that the entire eleven and eleven-twelfths years of his life had been one long struggle to get into the mainstream of life. Other people, he knew, were content with little pools on the sidelines, but he, he had always craved the thrill of the current.

But he hadn't wanted it yet! Not before he learned how to swim! He hadn't wanted to be pushed!

He began to question.

Once a person gets into the mainstream of life, can he ever get out? If he does get out, can he get back in? Or is it like an exclusive club: Once out, he must spend his remaining years on shore, watching the rest of the members swim by, thumbing their noses at—

"This is it, Worm Brain."

"Oh, sure."

Bingo braked and got off his bike. Together he and Wentworth walked toward the front door. Bingo said, "Er, Wentworth?"

"What?"

"Have you ever heard of something called the language of love?"

"No, what is it? A TV show?"

"No, it's like, well, it's a way you talk to girls."

"I got my own way."

"Yes, but mixed-sex conversations are different from regular conversations. I'm not saying I'm an expert, but I have had some successful ones."

"Listen, I could give *you* some advice on talking to girls. Now, get this. You stay behind me and don't say anything. We were just riding bikes down this street, see, and we pass her house, see, and naturally we think, Hey, maybe Cici don't know I'm back from vacation. We walk up the walk, see, like we're doing, and I ring the bell, like this. All you got to do is keep your mouth shut."

The door opened at once, and Cici peered around it. "Oh, hi, Bingo."

"I'm back from vacation," Wentworth said.

"Bingo, did it come? The letter?"

Bingo shook his head.

"Oh, when I saw you, I thought it had come and you were, like, bringing it back to me. I worry about that letter. When the mail comes, it's like panic time, you getting Melissa's letter, her getting yours. You promise it hasn't come?"

Bingo nodded.

Wentworth said again, "I'm back from vacation."

Now Cici looked at him. "So?"

"So if you've been wondering where I am, you don't have to wonder anymore."

"Bingo, let me know about the letter. Promise?"

Bingo nodded.

"Well, I've got to go. My mom and I are going to the Nautilus to pump iron. That's why I've got this on."

She stepped out like a model and showed them her pink stretch-knit exercise suit. "Taaa-daaaaaa!" Wentworth gasped and would have fallen over backward if Bingo had not grabbed him.

"Bye!"

And she was gone.

As they walked to their bikes, Wentworth said, "Now what was this language thing you were talking about?"

Two Helps in a Row

"Help!"

The call came again!

"Help!"

Then the scarlet water closed over the boy's head, and he found himself twisting downward in a tightening spiral toward the bowels of the earth.

Bingo was not starting a new science-fiction novel. Bingo was having a bad dream.

A faraway voice said, "Bingo." A hand shook him. "Wake up, Son."

Bingo opened his eyes. He was twisted into his sheet so tightly he could not move. The top sheet was damp with well-earned sweat.

"You must have been having a bad dream."

"A terrible undertow . . ." Bingo gasped. ". . . drowning . . ." He tried to twist free, but the Smurfs seemed to be clinging like leeches.

"Let me help you," his father said kindly.

"Thanks."

"Do you have drowning dreams often?" His dad continued to unwrap him as if he were unwrapping a mummy.

Bingo shook his head. "Just since I got in the mainstream of life."

"Yes, it's tough out here." His father smiled wryly. "Listen, Bingo, your mom wants to talk to you."

"Mom's home?"

"No, she's still at your grandmother's. She wants to talk to you on the phone."

Finally Bingo was free from his sheet. He got up. His notebook and pencil fell to the floor. The notebook fell open to a picture he had drawn weeks ago when, in his new maturity, he actually believed he had given up burning questions for all time and would never need the question mark again.

Bingo walked to the phone, bent forward, and took a deep breath. "Mom?"

"Bingo," his mother said in a rush, "listen, I'm sorry about the other night. That was a terrible thing to do, run out on your supper."

Bingo said, "Oh, well, it was just tuna lasagna."

"Now you'll never want to cook for me again."

"I'll cook again, but probably not lasagna."

"Are you all right? You aren't getting sick, are you, Bingo? You sound funny, as if you're far away."

"That's the way I feel."

"Did you just wake up?"

"Yes. I was having a terrible dream about the mainstream of life, which, incidentally, it appears I am now in."

"Well, go back to bed, Bingo. I'll talk to you later. I just wanted to apologize. I haven't been able to sleep for worrying about you."

"I'm worried about you, too." Bingo's father was in the doorway, listening. This reminded Bingo of why they were here in this awkward position. "Dad told me about your, er, problem. Maybe problem's not the right word. Maybe I should have said your difficulty, your"—he swallowed manfully—"pregnancy."

He went on in a rush. "Mom, if you'll come home tonight, I'll fix you the best supper you have ever had in your life. You name the recipe and I'll make it. I don't care what it is. I don't care how much the ingredients cost. Mom, I'll make it if you just tell me what it is and come on home."

"Bingo, I'm going to have to call you back. I can't deal with this right now."

"Mom—" Now his brain started working. "Mom, listen, I do feel funny. Maybe I am getting sick."

But she was gone.

He sat for a moment, holding the phone, and then he put it in its cradle. The mail was beside the phone, as if whoever had brought it in had abandoned it.

The top letter was to him. . . . Melissa.

He opened the flap without much enthusiasm and began to read.

Dear Bingo,
  I'm definitely worried now. I haven't heard from you in ages, and I can't help but wonder why.
  I should not have asked Cici to go to your

house and take your picture—I know that
now—because I remembered that one time I
was talking about you to Cici. I was telling
her about the time you and I went to the hospital to see Mr. Mark. I was saying you made
Mr. Mark laugh even though he begged you
not to. Anyway, that was when she said that
you sounded cute and she wished she knew
some cute boys.

Then, later, when I pointed you out to her
in the hall, she said you were cute and that
she wished she knew you. Now I guess she
does!

Please write me, Bingo, because I don't
know whether you want me to send my picture or not, so I won't put it in, but I'll keep
it in my stationery box.

                                Love (???)
                                Melissa

Bingo's dad came out of the bathroom then. "Bingo, I'm
not going to take time for breakfast. I want to stop by
your grandmother's on my way to work."

"I'll go with you." Bingo spun around. "It won't take
me a minute to get dressed." He had his pajamas almost
over his head before his father answered.

"That's not a good idea."

"Dad, wait! I have to tell Mom something. I just thought
of something to—"

"Call her back."

"Dad!

But his dad was gone.

"This is wrong!" Bingo picked up the telephone and slammed it down on the table. It gave its usual short ring of protest. "This is terribly wrong!"

He—*he* was supposed to leave the nest, and they—*they* were supposed to suffer from something called empty nest syndrome. Instead they—*they* had left him. And he—*he* had the disease. And it was an adult disease! How could someone eleven and eleven-twelfths be expected to handle an adult disease?

And—*and* how could they even consider having a second child when they had given their first a disease?

Sighing, he picked up the phone and dialed his grandmother's number. The phone rang so long he thought no one was going to answer. Then his mother's voice said cheerfully, "Hello."

She probably thought it was a real estate call. Bingo said with forced cheer, "Mom, hi. Sorry, it's just me again."

"Hi, Bingo."

"I just wondered if you'd had time to think about my offer, for supper."

"Not really."

"Mom, listen," he went on in a rush, "I don't want to say anything that will upset you, but have you ever heard of something called empty nest syndrome?"

"Yes."

"Well, I think I've got it."

"Bingo, Bingo, I'll come if I can."

And she was gone.

De Letter, Delivered

Bingo was making a sign for his bedroom window. It said DO NOT DISTURB. A threatening sketch completed the sign.

The necessity for a sign of this nature had become clear, because last night Wentworth had come over four times.

Finally, at this fourth interruption, Bingo had lost control.

"Wentworth," he had cried, "I've told you all I know about talking to girls. You talk to them like they're perfectly normal, everyday human beings and then suddenly—and, Wentworth, I don't know how this happens—but suddenly you're talking a different language. You're saying one thing and you're meaning another. There's a lot of eye contact involved. You can't do it looking down at your feet. You can't do it over the phone. Well, I can, but you can't. Now that is all I know!"

Bingo had gone back to bed and the series of burning questions that had been troubling him.

When I am a man, if something goes wrong with my

life, one of those cruel U-turns of fate like my mom had,
will I want to come home like my mom? Will I want to
sleep in this bed? What color will the Smurfs be then?

Will I be able to come home? Won't there be a child in
this room? In this bed? On these Smurf sheets?

At last Bingo had fallen into a troubled sleep.

Now it was morning, and making the sign made Bingo
feel better. At last he was doing something positive.

He put away his magic markers and set the sign in the
window. Then he went outside to see how it would look
to someone ready to knock.

Arms crossed, head to the side, he judged his work. Any
person in their right mind, seeing such a sign, would not
knock, but then . . .

Shaking his head, he started back into the house. He
was at the steps when the mailman handed him the letters.
The top letter was for him.

It was another letter from Melissa. One yesterday, now
one today, and both on top.

Bingo thought it was as if Melissa's letters rose to the

surface, as if they were lighter than bills and junk mail, because they were always on top, always.

It didn't make him love her again, but still he admitted Melissa's letters were probably the nicest things the post office had to offer.

He turned the envelope over. On the back was written:

Deliver
De letter
De sooner
De better
De later
De letter
De madder
I getter

Bingo sighed. Now he knew he no longer loved Melissa.

As a writer, words were naturally important to Bingo. He was affected deeply by what people wrote. He had once fallen out of love with a girl named Mamie Lou just because she had written a letter to Laura Ingalls Wilder that said, "I know that you are dead, but please write if you can and tell me where you get your ideas."

And, Bingo thought, he was especially affected by what people wrote on the backs of envelopes.

Yes, he no longer loved Melissa. Regretfully, he opened the flap. As he took out the letter, he smelled the fragrance of an unfamiliar flower.

Then he saw the heading: *"From the Desk of Cici"*
Cici!

Bingo drew in a deep breath. He should have known,

but he was in such a state of personal agitation that he was blind to what was going on around him. In his agitated blindness, he had fallen out of love with a girl he had never been in love with!

This was the letter! *The* letter!

Bingo closed his eyes. If the first words in *the* letter were "Dear Melissa," then he was honor bound—*honor bound*—to put it back in the envelope without reading it.

Even though this would mean that he would never know what Cici wrote to Melissa—and it had to be something about him—maybe even something hurtful. Maybe something to make Melissa fall out of love with him! And even though he was out of love with Melissa, he did not want her to fall out of love with him.

If his eyes—when he opened them—saw two words, "Dear Melissa," then he would have to—be honor bound to—put the letter back in the envelope.

He opened his eyes. "Dear Melissa." Bingo read faster.

> I got his picture!
> I went to his house. He opened the door himself! He said, "Hi," and smiled. I was so blissed out that I honestly didn't mind he had freckles! He held the door open. I almost died! I went into his living room *and* into his kitchen. Melissa, guess what? He'd been cooking! In an apron!
> We went out in the backyard. He smiled. I took his picture. Melissa, I was so blissed out I got my thumb in front of the lens. He smiled

again. I took another picture. Then a terrible
thing happened. This nerd next door stuck his
head over the hedge. Bingo and I had to go in
the house to get rid of him.

We went in the kitchen. He put on his
apron, and he looked sooo cute. We started
talking. I was holding a poodle. He was cooking. We were having a blast!

Then—booo—something really awful happened. His mom came home. I was hoping
she'd say, "Stay for supper," but she didn't.
She freaked out. Like, the whole time I was
explaining why I was there, her eyes were
shooting darts at me. Finally she goes, "Bingo
is not allowed to have friends in the house
when either his father or I"—blah, blah, blah.

I hope you like the picture. I kept one for
myself, the one of him with the poodle. I love
that dog.

Bingo bent closer. It looked to him as if the word "dog"
had originally been "boy." She had originally written, "I
love that boy." The *d* had been a *b!* The *g* had been a *y!*
Bingo could see it plain as day. He bent to read the rest.

Write and tell me if you like the picture I
took for you. I'll go over to his house as often
as I can so I'll have lots of interesting things
to write you about.

Your #1 friend,
Cici

The two *i*'s had hearts over them instead of dots.

Bingo's photo had fluttered unnoticed from the envelope to the floor. Now he picked it up and looked at it with new intensity.

He went directly to the bathroom. He stood looking at himself in the mirror.

Could this be the face that two girls loved?

His eyes gazed first at the face in the mirror, then at the face in the photograph. Could there be something in this face that he did not see? What was it? Where was it?

And one final burning question: How long would it last?

The Black-Belt Eyebrow

Bingo was looking into the dim recesses of the medicine cabinet. He had noticed last week that the Yogi Bear vitamins were gone. Bingo shook the can of mousse. They were out of that, too.

Every drugstore product that had brought him comfort in the past had been swept from the cabinet as he himself had been swept from the family. He wouldn't have been surprised to find himself actually gone, vanished.

He turned the cabinet door around and peered in the mirror. No, he was still there.

As Bingo was closing the cabinet, giving up, his eyes spotted an unfamiliar container. He reached for it at once.

Perhaps this bottle had been there all along behind the mousse, he thought. Perhaps it was a product that his parents had even concealed behind the mousse.

He took it in his hand and read the unfamiliar words: Skin Bracer.

Well, everything about him needed bracing, Bingo thought, that was for sure. Might as well start with the skin. He applied the skin bracer to both cheeks and waited.

His skin was not braced. Maybe his skin was a little cooler. It certainly smelled better, but Bingo could not say it was braced.

Bingo decided to do something he had never done before—read the directions.

"Apply after shaving," the directions said.

Bingo drew in his breath.

After shaving!

Bingo felt these were probably the two most important words he had ever read in his life. He was so moved he had to close his eyes and hold onto the basin for support.

He clung for a moment, head down, knuckles whitening. Then, slowly, he raised his head and had eye contact with himself.

For days Bingo had felt like the helpless victim of the entire world, a toy in the turbulent mainstream of life. Now, at last, he could do something positive for himself. With one stroke of the razor, he could put childhood behind him forever.

Bingo reached for his father's razor, swallowed, and clicked it on.

The ensuing buzz was the most comforting sound Bingo

had ever heard. He rubbed the razor tentatively over his chin. Then his cheeks.

Bingo moved with special care over his upper lip, where, for all he knew, a latent mustache lay below the surface.

Then he went over his sideburns; they were latent, too. In his eagerness, he even took off a little bit of one eyebrow.

Then Bingo clicked off the razor and stepped back for the result.

It took his breath away.

His face was—he loved this description—clean shaven.

He actually liked himself better without that part of his eyebrow. And—and! It gave him a quizzical look, as if he questioned the very nature of existence—which he did.

He looked at his reflection for a long time, turning this way and that. Finally satisfied, he reached for the skin bracer.

Bingo splashed it on liberally. It was bracing! It was so bracing it stung. It actually brought tears to Bingo's eyes.

The phone rang.

Blinking back well-deserved tears, Bingo went to the phone and picked it up.

Fortunately the phone had a long cord so Bingo could take the phone back into the bathroom and watch himself in the mirror as he talked.

"Hell-o!" This was the first cheerful hello he had heard from himself in months.

"Bingo, it's your dad."

"Oh, hi."

"Are you busy?"

"Not really."

"Well, listen, what say we get some flowers and go see your mom?"

Bingo lifted his shortened eyebrow quizzically. He loved it. He loved it! He looked like a famous rock star. He looked like—

"Bingo, are you there?"

"Yes."

Bingo brought the eyebrow down. It looked good down, too! Down it was a suggestive snarl, like the curl of Elvis Presley's lip. But up! Up it turned him into a totally different person. Up! Down! Yes, up was better, but down wasn't shabby.

"Bingo, what are you doing?"

"Nothing. Nothing, Dad. I'm not doing anything. I'm talking to you."

"Well, I'll get the flowers, Bingo, and pick you up in, oh, a half hour."

"I"—up—"will be waiting." Up! Up!

The last two ups gave Bingo a sobering thought.

Now that he had this eyebrow, he would have to use its powers as carefully as a person with a black belt. Perhaps even have cards printed up. "Warning: The bearer of this card has a black belt in eyebrow."

Bingo smiled. With one final up/down, he backed reluctantly away from the bathroom mirror.

Hot Dog Surprise

Bingo sat beside his father in the car. His father's flowers, a dozen yellow roses, were in a box on the back seat.

On Bingo's lap was a small casserole, Hot Dog Surprise, although Bingo knew the hot dogs weren't going to be much of a surprise, since they were now sticking up through the grated cheese.

When Bingo's dad had proposed taking the flowers to his mom, Bingo had been so exhilarated by his new eyebrow that he had not questioned the wisdom of the plan. He had rushed directly into the kitchen, whipped open *The Three Ingredient Cookbook,* thrown together Hot Dog Surprise, and gone out on the front steps.

He had sat on the steps, smiling in anticipation of their triumph.

Now, gazing down at the small unappealing casserole, Bingo realized how doomed the plan was.

Burning questions plagued him as they sped toward his grandmother's condo.

Was this his role in life, to accompany the less fortunate on doomed missions of the heart? First Wentworth, now his own father? Was he himself doomed to share the stupidity of others forever? Was this the price one paid for skill in the language of love? Was—

They pulled up in front of the condo. Bingo could see his face in the side mirror as he got out of the car. His face was so flushed he could not see his freckles, but he knew they were there. "Freckles are forever," his father had told him once.

Even his new eyebrow seemed to have lost some of its power. It just looked like a shortened version of his other eyebrow.

Bingo and his father made their way up the walk. His dad was holding the box of roses over his arm like a bridesmaid would. Bingo held his casserole in front of him.

Bingo's dad rang the bell.

"They're not here," Bingo said immediately.

"Give them a chance."

His father rang again. His grandmother's doorbell was one of those cheerful, uplifting ding-dong ones, but Bingo was neither cheered nor uplifted.

They waited in silence. Bingo shifted his weight to one hip.

"We look stupid," Bingo said bluntly.

"Sometimes you have to risk looking stupid to get what you want," his father answered in a mild way. "More people have lost out on more good things because they were afraid of looking stupid. . . ."

He rang the bell twice. *Ding dong! Ding dong!*

Bingo passed the time alternately hoping that his mother would come to the door and that she wouldn't. He wanted to see her and he didn't want to see her. He found he couldn't remember exactly what she looked like.

Bingo shifted his weight to the other hip. He sighed. He felt that an unfortunate pattern was being established in his life.

"Is this what it's like when you go on dates?"

"What?"

"Is this what it's like to go on dates? You know, standing out here and not knowing if she's coming to the door, not knowing if you even want her to come, wondering if you'll recognize her, wondering if she's hiding in the closet, waiting for you to leave, wondering if you've got time to run and hide in the bushes."

"At first, I guess."

"Then I shall never go on dates."

"You'll change your mind when you fall in love," his father said, punching the bell again.

Bingo rolled his eyes up into his head at this parental blindness.

"Actually, it was worse in college."

Bingo glanced quickly at his dad. "How could it be any worse than this?"

"Well, they had a loudspeaker system at Catawba. So they'd call up to your date's floor and say, 'Sam Brown to see so-and-so,' and you'd be standing there all dressed up, obviously expecting to go out, and the loudspeaker would come back with, 'Sorry! So-and-so's not here.' "

"How cruel!"

"Even if it didn't happen to you, you were always aware it could."

"Maybe I won't go to Catawba College after all," Bingo added thoughtfully. "Did Mom ever do that to you?"

"No, your mom was in love with me. Half the time she'd be waiting for me outside on the steps."

Melissa would have been waiting for me like that, Bingo thought regretfully, that is, if my love had lasted till college.

His father rang the bell for what Bingo sincerely hoped was the last *ding dong.* He glanced down at his casserole.

His father gave up. "We'll just leave the flowers on the stoop, if that's all right with you."

"It is."

"I'll write a note."

His father clicked open his pen. They had not thought to get a card, so he had to write on the top of the box.

Bingo wanted to tell his father that something called the language of love might be needed here, ordinary words that portrayed extraordinary emotions.

Bingo's dad finished. "You want to sign it?"

Bingo read it. The note said, "We love you and miss you and want you to come home. Sam."

Well, they were ordinary words, that was for sure, but Bingo couldn't detect a trace of the language of love.

He took the pen and added: *"Cook at 350 until hot and bubbly. Your faithful son, Bingo Brown"*

His father laid the box of roses on the stoop as solemnly as if he were laying a wreath in a cemetery. Bingo put his casserole on top.

Then, together, they walked in silence to the car.

CUT SMUT!

Bingo's grandmother was, as he knew she would be, in front of the convenience store. There were eight other women, one with a baby, and two men. His grandmother was the only one in an appropriate T-shirt. Two weeks ago, in happier times, Bingo had designed it himself. It was one word, "SMUT," with the "not allowed" sign printed over it.

He had also helped his grandmother make the two signs that she now held so proudly.

One of the signs read:

```
CLEAN AIR
CLEAN WATER
CLEAN MINDS
CLEAN EARTH
```

The other:

> UNLESS WE LEAVE THE WORLD BETTER THAN
> WE FOUND IT, THERE IS NO JUSTIFICATION FOR
> OUR EXISTENCE.

"The letters will have to be real little," Bingo had warned her as he blocked out the second sign.

"I don't care. It's my motto in life."

"People won't be able to read it from across the street."

She had held up her red T-shirt with the huge unallowed "SMUT" on it. "Well, they'll be able to read that, won't they?"

She had looked critically at herself in the mirror, with the T-shirt against her. Bingo had watched.

After a minute she had said, "I will do anything, including make a fool of myself, to make this world a cleaner, better place."

Bingo loved his grandmother. She was almost exactly like his mother. They both wore their hair pulled back, they both wore the same size clothes, they both wore Pure Watermelon lipstick. The only things different were that his grandmother was a little bit more wrinkled and that she had no faults whatsoever.

Bingo called her Grammy, like the award.

Grammy was a person, Bingo thought now, who would never run away from her child and husband, no matter what misfortune befell her.

For a moment Bingo remained in the shadows of Video

Village, watching his beloved grandmother. Video Village had been picketed by CUT! in the spring, and they now displayed a sign in the window saying, "We no longer carry X-rated films."

His grandmother's head was turned toward the store, but as a car went by, she swirled and, face bright with hope, began to lead a cheer.

> Two, Four, Six, Eight
> It's smut we hate!
> Two, Four, Six, Eight
> It's—

Slowly Bingo crossed the street. "Harrison!" His grandmother broke off her cheer. She was the only person in the world who called him by his real name.

She embraced him so vigorously that her protest signs flapped around his ears. "Are you joining us? Are you going to help us protest?"

"Not really, Grammy," Bingo said. "I just wanted to talk to you."

"Here, hold this while we talk." She pressed the Clean Air sign into his hand. "You can look as if you're protesting even if you aren't. We need some young people."

"I'll be glad to." Bingo took the sign, but it drooped. He held it as if he intended to hit a golf ball with it instead of protest.

"Now what did you want to talk about?"

"Did Mom get my casserole last night?" Bingo asked. "I had to leave it on the front stoop. I was afraid a dog or cat might—"

"She got it."

"I guess you were out, since you didn't come to the door."

"Yes, we went out for pizza."

"You didn't eat the casserole?"

"We're saving it for tonight."

"Oh. Did Dad's flowers do any good?"

His grandmother hugged him with her free arm. "Every act of kindness does good, Harrison." She smiled. "Your mother needs your support right now."

"Well, I need hers. Doesn't she know that?"

"She knows. Sometimes a person needs a little extra support."

"You can say that again."

She hugged him.

"Grammy, will you let her know that I forgive her for what she did?"

"Harrison . . ." Her voice was low, as if she were chiding him, but since she had never chided him before in his entire life, that could not be possible.

"I forgive her even though when this baby is my age, I'll be twenty-four."

"So what? I'll be seventy-four."

His grandmother broke off the conversation. A car was turning into the 7-11 parking lot. His grandmother moved forward to take her place at the head of the protesters.

Inspired, the others broke into a new chant:

> *Smut no more! Smut no more!*
> *Starting with this convenience store!*
> *Smut no more! Smut no more!*

Bingo's grandmother signaled the driver to roll down his window. She did this with a gesture worthy of a highway patrolman.

"What's going on here?" the driver asked.

"Sir, we're asking the people of Townsville to boycott this store until the manager agrees to remove pornographic magazines from the shelves. Will you help us?"

The man hesitated. "I was just going to get a loaf of bread."

"Yes, but that loaf of bread can make Townsville a better place for your children."

The driver shifted gears and, with a sigh, circled the gas pumps and drove out of the parking lot, accompanied by cheers. Even Bingo raised his sign.

"When's Mom coming home?" he asked.

"I'm working on it."

"Do you think it'll be tonight? Because I'd like to fix something special. That casserole last night, that was just something I got from *The Three Ingredient Cookbook*."

"Probably not tonight."

"You could come, too. Grammy, I just realized you've never tasted my cooking."

The lady with the baby had stepped up beside Bingo, and Bingo felt a light tap on his shoulder.

He glanced around and saw that he was being patted by the tiniest hand he had ever seen in his life. He had not known hands came that tiny. This baby—of all people in the world—this baby, a stranger to him, this baby had sensed the depth of his anguish and had reached out. It was like a message of hope from the future.

He hadn't known babies brought comfort! He only thought they had to be comforted, changed, pacified. This was a whole new concept.

"Harrison, hold your sign up!"

"What?" The tiny hand was holding his shirt now. Bingo could not move. He was held in place as surely as if the hand that held him was made of iron.

"That's the WAXA television truck. It's turning in! We're going to be on TV!"

She grabbed Bingo's arm and thrust it high into the air. He quickly repositioned the sign over his face and hid behind it.

The baby let go.

A Thief at the Mailbox

Bingo rounded the corner slowly. His cheeks still felt hot from the strain of participating in the protest.

Although he had tried to hold the Clean Air sign directly in front of his face the whole time the TV truck was there, he might have—in fact he was pretty sure he had—peered around the sign twice. He might—in fact he was pretty sure he would—be on the evening news.

And worst of all, it had been the side of his face without the new clipped eyebrow! From now on he would have to be as careful about which side of his face was photographed as a movie star.

He looked up at his house and stopped. His lower jaw dropped in astonishment. Billy Wentworth was on Bingo's porch, putting something in Bingo's mailbox. What was going on here?

Bingo moved closer. Then he saw that Wentworth was

not putting something into his mailbox! He was taking something out!

Billy Wentworth was stealing their mail!

Silently, moving in a line so straight it could have been drawn with a ruler, Bingo closed the distance between himself and Wentworth. Now he, Bingo, was Rambo, and Billy Wentworth the hapless victim. Now Billy Wentworth would know what it was like to be ambushed!

Wentworth never heard a sound, never suspected a thing. He was staring at the envelope in his hand as if he were hypnotized, as if he couldn't believe what he saw.

Bingo said in a loud voice, "Stealing people's mail is a criminal offense."

At that Wentworth spun around. He had the grace to look momentarily embarrassed.

"This isn't mail."

"It was in my mailbox."

"It still isn't mail—no stamp."

Wentworth turned the envelope around so Bingo could see for himself.

"If it's in the mailbox, it's mail," Bingo said coldly. In a lightning-quick gesture he whipped the envelope from Wentworth's fingers and went into the house.

Wentworth opened the door and started to follow, but Bingo gave him a cool glance and a quick raise of the new eyebrow. Wentworth stopped in place.

"Look," Wentworth explained. "That girl. Remember?" He swallowed and said hoarsely, "Cici? Well, I saw her over here, putting a letter in your mailbox, all right? And

I thought maybe she'd got our houses mixed up and the letter was for me. I just wanted to make absolutely sure the letter was for you instead of me."

"All right, you've made absolutely sure." Bingo looked at the envelope. He took a long time to read his own name. "Mr. Bingo Brown. Yes, I believe that's me."

"What does the letter say?"

"Well, I would have to open it to find that out, wouldn't I?"

Bingo slid the envelope into his back pocket with a deliberate motion.

Wentworth swallowed again. Bingo thought he was working up the strength to say the emotion-filled word "Cici" again, but Wentworth was getting ready to come up with an even harder word, one Bingo was not aware was part of Wentworth's vocabulary.

"Please."

Bingo looked at Billy Wentworth while time ticked away. Then, like an actor, still looking into Wentworth's rapidly blinking eyes, Bingo reached into his back pocket.

Wentworth tried to move closer to Bingo so they could read the letter together, but with a quick lift of the black-belt eyebrow, Bingo stopped him.

He opened the envelope slowly. "From the desk of Cici," he read.

He read the next few lines to himself.

"Would you mind reading it aloud, please," Billy Wentworth said.

Bingo read:

"Dear Bingo,

I know now that you got Melissa's letter!
The reason I know is because, like, she got
yours!

She freaked out at me for writing you, and
she told me she didn't want to be my best
friend anymore. She goes, 'With a best friend
like you, I don't need any enemies!' "

Bingo paused, and Billy Wentworth made a rolling gesture with his hand, indicating he would like to hear more.

"I doubt if it gets any better," Bingo said, "but if you
want to hear it . . ." He shrugged and read on.

"Please write Melissa! Tell her *nothing happened* between us.

If you want to talk to me about this, you
can come over to my house right away. I will
be waiting!

Or you can call me at the number below!
                Sincerely (and hopefully),
                                    Cici"

"What does this mean?" Wentworth pointed with one
dirty finger to the line, "Tell her *nothing happened* between
us."

"It means for me to tell Melissa that nothing happened
between us."

"And did anything happen between you?"

"No."

"You're sure about that?"

"Positive."

"Could I read the letter for myself?"

"Why would you want to?"

"I don't know. I just do."

Bingo handed over the letter, and Billy Wentworth read it, word by word. "She uses little hearts to dot the *i*'s in her name," he said.

"I saw that."

Billy Wentworth looked up. Bingo thought of the way Pepe Le Pew looks in cartoons when he falls in love with a lady skunk. Hearts actually radiate out of his eyes. That was the pitiable way Wentworth looked now.

"So are you going?" Wentworth asked.

"Where?"

"Over to her house."

"Of course not."

"Why?"

"Because I don't want to."

"Can I go in your place?"

"What for?"

"To, you know, let her know you're not coming."

"Do whatever you like. Good-bye, Wentworth."

With that, Bingo turned on his heels and went directly to his room. He reached under his bed for his notebook. He turned to a new page. He began to write.

Trials of Today
(minor)
Triumphs of Today
(major!)

1. I no longer fear Wentworth.
2. I have created a black-belt eyebrow that will take me far.
3. I may have a cameo television appearance on the six o'clock news.
4. I have felt a baby's touch.
5. I am at last putting childhood behind me.

With five good solid Triumphs to his credit, he decided to start a new category.

Goals for Tomorrow

1. Becoming a man.

Play It Again, Bingo

Bingo was sitting on the edge of the sofa cushion, watching the evening news. He was waiting for the electric moment when his face would—or perhaps mercifully would not—appear on the screen. Outside, a lawn mower droned as Billy Wentworth moved back and forth across the grass.

The announcer said, "On the local scene . . ."

With his thumbs, Bingo pressed the tape buttons on the VCR remote control. The tape began to roll with a hum. Bingo's heart speeded up.

". . . members of CUT!—Clean Up Townsville!—today picketed a local convenience store on—"

At that moment a knock came at the front door.

"I'm busy!" Bingo called without taking his eyes from the TV screen.

Another knock.

"Wentworth, if that's you—"

"It's not. It's me, Cici."

"Well, I can't talk now. I'm on TV."

"Oh, Bingo, where? Let me see."

Before Bingo could stop her, Cici was inside the house. She stood, back against the door, her hands clasped beneath her chin.

Her attitude was so prayerful that Bingo didn't have the heart to make her back out onto the porch and watch his TV appearance through the screen.

They watched in silence. Then Bingo gasped. "That's me. Right there, behind the Clean Air sign!"

"I recognize your hands!"

"Thank you."

"And the top of your head! That's the top of *your* head!"

"My grandmother's in the Smut T-shirt. I made that for her."

"Oh, I didn't know that was your grandmother. Bingo, the announcer's going to ask your grandmother a question! Your grandmother's going to be on TV! She's—"

He cut off her piercing voice with a gesture he had learned from Billy Wentworth.

In the silence that followed, his grandmother said she was proud that the people of Townsville supported the picketing and she was especially proud "that some of our fine young people are supporting us, too."

Here she placed one hand on the top of Bingo's head.

"What's next for CUT!?" the announcer asked.

"For far too long," his grandmother said sternly, "local residents have been dumping waste material into Bohicket Creek. It's become a joke. CUT! intends to turn Bohicket Creek into the garden spot of the county."

There was applause from the group, one last shot of the infamous convenience store, and the scene faded away.

"Area dairy farmers," the announcer continued, "are becoming increasingly concerned about the drought, and here's Chuck Wertz, our weatherman, to tell us if there's any relief in sight. Chuck?"

Bingo pressed the stop button on the VCR, and Cici blinked her eyes rapidly.

Bingo recognized that Cici was thinking, probably trying to remember why she had come over.

As Bingo waited, he remembered with a pang how thrilling it had been to watch Melissa think. When Melissa thought, she lifted her head. That was it. But when she lifted her head—and Bingo knew she didn't do this on purpose; if she'd done it on purpose it wouldn't have been nearly as thrilling—when she lifted her head, it made Bingo think that some low-minded opportunist, like himself, could catch her by surprise and press his lips against—

"Why are your eyes closed?" Cici asked.

"They weren't."

"Yes, they were, and you were leaning forward like you were getting ready to—"

"I was not!"

"—pass out," she finished.

Bingo took a deep breath. "I did feel a little woozy," he admitted.

There was a knock at the door. "Anybody home?" Wentworth asked innocently. He opened the door and came in the living room. His shorts, combat boots, and naked skin were flecked with sweat and grass clippings.

"Hi, Cici," he said. He took off his wraparound dark glasses.

"Hi," Cici said without enthusiasm.

"What are you guys up to?"

"Nothing, we were just watching Bingo on TV," Cici said.

"What was the Worm Brain doing on TV?"

Bingo realized suddenly that Billy Wentworth was the only boy he knew who sweated like a man. Bingo knew too that Wentworth did not—and probably never would—use deodorant. He knew this for a fact.

"Enemy attack dogs," Wentworth had told the class once last year. It was an assignment on little-known facts. Bingo could see him now, standing at parade rest, announcing in the voice of a sergeant, "Enemy attack dogs have keen senses of smell and are trained to seek out and attack Right Guard, Brut, Arrid Extra Dry, Mennon's Stick, and Five-Day Underarm Deodorant Pads."

This was such a little-known fact that even their teacher, Mr. Mark, had not heard of it. "Where do you come up with these things, Billy?"

"Training manuals."

The class had sat in awed silence, with their arms pressed tightly at their sides. On his way back to his seat, Wentworth told them, "So don't say I didn't warn you."

Bingo now felt he had to somehow get it across to Wentworth that before you could even attempt the language of love, you had to smell worthy of it. Bingo felt he was up to this task now that he had the eyebrow for it.

Billy Wentworth stepped closer to Cici. He said, "I was going to come over to your house later."

"What for?" Cici asked, blinking her eyes.

"To tell you Bingo wasn't coming over, but now that you're here, I can tell you now. Bingo's not coming over."

Cici stepped closer to Bingo and said, "Let's see it again, please."

"Well, all right." Bingo rewound the tape. "Though you really couldn't see much of me."

"I could," Cici said. "I saw both your hands *and* the top of your head."

"I wasn't sure *both* my hands were on . . ."

"Play it again, Bingo," Cici said.

"Well, all right." Bingo pressed the play button and waited, eyes on the screen, for the group in front of the convenience store to appear. He turned off the sound and began his own commentary. "That's me . . . behind the Clean Air sign . . . that's my right hand, but you can only see two fingers of my—"

"Wait," Cici said. Then in a different, deeper voice, she cried, "Oh, Bingo, look! There's a little baby's hand on your shoulder. A tiny little baby is patting you."

Cici was so moved by this that she threw one arm around Bingo's neck and began to jump up and down.

The suddenness and violence of the attack—there could be no other word for it—made Bingo feel he was the helpless victim of a force of nature, a tornado or an earthquake or one of those baboons that kill their mates by twisting off their heads.

His desperate thoughts were interrupted by his mother's voice. She spoke coolly from the doorway.

"And just what is going on here?"

Bingo's Father-Mother

"I don't know how these things happen to me!" Bingo cried as soon as Wentworth and Cici had left. "Mom, I have a very simple, sometimes a pitifully simple life. Sometimes it's even as if I'm the victim of life, and then—and this always happens just before you appear—some sort of cruel twist of fate occurs, and I seem to be doing something I am not doing, something I have no intention of doing, something I would never do in my own living room. I know exactly what you're thinking. You're thinking I invited this girl over, aren't you? You're thinking I called her up and said, 'Look, my mom is pregnant and has walked out on me and my dad, so this would be a good time for you to come over. We can have the house to ourselves.' Is that what you think of me? Because if that's what you think of me, then I want you to say, 'Yes, that's what I think of you, Bingo.' And after that I'm going to go over to Grammy's. You're not the only one who can desert the family, you know."

"Are you through?" his mom said.

"For the moment."

"You're quite wrong, you know."

"About what?"

"About what I think of you."

"Oh?"

"I think you're terrific."

"Huh!"

"It's true."

"Then why—tell me this—why did your eyes get very little when you looked at me? The answer is that your eyes always get very little when you look at something you don't like. So when I see little eyes that means one thing. Mom does not like—"

"Oh, Bingo, don't let's fight. I'm too happy to fight."

Bingo stopped in midsentence. "You're happy?"

"Yes." She sat down on the sofa.

"What about?"

"Oh, the baby."

"I didn't think you were happy about the baby. Otherwise, why would you run away from home?"

"I didn't run away, Bingo. I went to spend some time with my mother. It always helps me to talk to Mom."

"It looked like running away."

"Well, anyway, I am very happy now. For once in my life, Bingo, everything is going to work out the way it should."

"It is?"

"Look, here's the situation. I love my job. Bingo, I can really sell real estate. I can't tell you how happy it makes me to have something I like to do and that I'm good at."

She breathed in some new air.

"Your father has never liked his job. You are aware of that, aren't you, Bingo?"

Bingo nodded.

"Selling insurance just isn't what he should be doing. Your father's a very sensitive and creative man. In college he always wanted to be a writer, and lately he's started getting back to it. Your dad's writing a novel, Bingo."

Bingo gasped. "Are you sure it's a novel? It looked more like a short story to me."

"It's a novel—sort of a funny crime novel. Anyway, after the baby comes, your dad can stay home and write. I can work."

"Does Dad know about this?"

"Bingo, your dad suggested it himself! He will be a house husband, and— Oh, Bingo, it just made me appreciate him so much, and your little casserole made me appreciate you so much, and it made me feel that I was the only one in the family who wasn't acting mature and terrific."

"Well, actually, I wasn't going to say anything, but since you brought it up—"

The phone rang then, stopping Bingo.

"I'll get it," his mom said. Then, "They have accepted the offer? Wonderful! . . . Yes . . . . Well, I can pick you up right now. . . . Yes, I'll see you in fifteen minutes."

"Mom—"

"I've got to wash my face and run, Bingo."

His mother went into the bathroom, and Bingo went directly into his parents' room to the typewriter. He wanted to read his father's novel. There were only six pages. Bingo got them in order.

"My father, Lewis," Bingo read, "had five wives, but I was his only child, so it was up to me to bust him out of jail."

Was this a novel? Would anybody want to read a novel that started out like that?

His mom had to be mistaken. He leafed through the pages until he came to the title page.

"*Bustin' Lewis,* a novel by Sam Brown."

Bingo heard his mother in the hall, and he dropped his father's novel. "Mom?" he called quickly.

She came to the bedroom door. "What is it?"

"There's something important I've got to ask you. I've been wondering about this ever since I heard about the baby."

"Go ahead."

"Will the same doctor be delivering this baby that delivered me?"

"Yes."

"Well, Mom, when this baby pops out, if the doctor says, 'Bingo' again, he's not naming the baby."

Breaking into a smile, she said, "I'll keep that in mind."

"One Bingo is enough."

Still smiling, she said, "I don't know about that."

"Mom!"

"There'll never be a Bingo Two."

She threw this over her shoulder as she went out onto the porch.

The words and the bright way she said them caused Bingo's face to flush, as if he were close to a warm fire.

Later that evening an unflushed Bingo opened his journal. He wrote thoughtfully.

Triumphs of Today

1. Attaining the mainstream of life and, despite the unexpected strength of the current, not paddling in panic for shore.

2. Accepting calmly the thought of having my father for my mother.

3. Continuing to go over *Bustin' Lewis* and realizing that if my father needs my help in his writing career, I will give it willingly and unselfishly.

Trials of Today: none!

The Mainstream of Bingo's Life

Melissa's letter wasn't on top of the mail this afternoon. It was sandwiched between two sweepstakes entries, so Bingo didn't get it until after supper.

"Letter!" his mother called, sailing it into his room as if it were a Frisbee. Since it was not a Frisbee, it only fluttered a few feet into the room.

Bingo got up from the bed to retrieve it. Bingo's mother was in a wonderful mood. In the past week she had sold a condo and had a contract on a Tudor split-level.

His dad was in even better spirits. It was as if becoming a house husband and a writer had been his lifelong ambitions. He had two chapters done on *Bustin' Lewis* now. So far, Bingo had not had a chance to step in with editorial advice, but he was ready to do so at any time.

Yes, Bingo noticed, his parents were acting like high school teenagers going to a prom. He alone was acting in a restrained manner. It seemed to him that his new manliness should be especially obvious in the midst of the childish actions of his parents. Still, no one had commented on it so far.

Bingo waited until his mother left the doorway before he opened the letter. Even with his new manliness, he had not reached the point where he could read letters without making facial expressions. Sometimes his mouth dropped open, sometimes his eyes popped, sometimes he had to put his hand over his heart.

Until he conquered his facial muscles, it was best to read in private.

Bingo opened the letter, but before he could unfold it, he noticed a picture fluttering to the floor—just as his own picture had fluttered from Cici's letter.

Burning questions flared like fireworks.

Was Melissa returning his picture? Wasn't it good enough? Had he used too much mousse? Too little? What was the trouble?

Bingo picked up the picture and held it to the light.

Melissa.

It was a picture of Melissa.

And she was looking right at him. It was as if the camera were a device that allowed people hundreds of miles apart to have eye contact with each other.

Bingo was so dazzled that he closed his eyes and rested the picture against his ribs. When he was almost under control, he looked at it again.

He marveled at it.

Just two months in Bixby, Oklahoma, had done this to Melissa! Two months in Bixby, Oklahoma, had turned her into the most beautiful person in the entire world!

Her hair had always been jazzy, but now, Bingo thought, in Bixby, Oklahoma, it had thrived. It was longer, curlier, shinier. It was—this was the first time Bingo had ever used the word—luxurious. Her hair was luxurious enough to be in a mousse ad!

Bingo knew that from now on, every time he heard the word luxurious, he would think of Melissa's hair. When he was ninety-two, if someone said, "Isn't the foliage luxurious this summer?" he would nod, but his brain would soar with the thought of Melissa's hair.

He broke off to marvel at her smile.

Melissa's smile had always made his heart beat faster. It, too, was jazzy. But now it had gotten so beautiful that it made his stomach— He was pretty sure it had been his stomach that had attempted a flip on Melissa's porch that rainy afternoon, because now it was attempting another one.

Bingo put his hand over his stomach and patted it in a calming way. It could not possibly be good for a stomach to be jumping out of place. Bingo would just as soon it didn't do that.

Anyway, it was back in place now, so Bingo had reason to hope that no permanent damage had been done.

He bent over the picture.

Had her teeth always been that white? And they weren't big horse teeth like some girls had; they were small and squarish except for two, one on each side, that were small and pointed. Bingo never had cared for long teeth.

Her eyes . . . She was squinting a little with one eye because of the sun, and Bingo had never seen her squint before. He hadn't known how beautiful her squint would be.

His stomach attempted another flip, and Bingo thought he better stop looking at this picture for a minute.

He lay back on his bed with the picture propped against his chest.

When his body was working normally again, Bingo reached under the bed for his summer journal. He tore out seven sheets of paper. Bingo had a lot to say.

"Dear Melissa," he began. The words poured from him.

> I am going to be a brother. At first, Melissa, I was not happy about this; after all, I will be 24 when the child is my age, but with the unresponsible way my parents have been acting lately—my mother went home to her mother for a while, and my father is going to become my mother—well, it seems to me this child may need an older brother, one into maturity. I feel now that it may be up to me to help this child reach the mainstream of life, as I have only recently done myself.
>
> If I can do this, sparing him—or her—some of the difficult experiences I have undergone in attaining that mainstream, then big brotherhood will not be, as they say, in vain.
>
> In addition to this challenge, I am preparing to help my father with his comic/crime novel,

Bustin' Lewis, if that becomes necessary, and
I am continuing to help Wentworth, who
knows nothing of the language of love (which
you and I put to such good use on your porch
when we said good-bye).

It is true that Cici has been over at my house
too much. However, seeing her has only made
me realize how much better it would be to see
you. Just yesterday Cici was standing there,
blinking her eyes, thinking (I suppose), and I
remembered how thrilling it was to watch you
think.

Melissa, when you think, you sort of lift
your head, and when you lift your head like
that—I know you don't do this on purpose;
if you did it on purpose it wouldn't be nearly
as thrilling—when you lift your head, and I
hope you won't think I am a low-minded
opportunist, but when you lift your head,
I . . .

Bingo stopped.

Melissa's letter! He had forgotten the letter. He hadn't
even read it.

He unfolded the letter and spread it flat on his knees. It
was on pale blue paper, the same color as the T-shirt she
had worn so effectively last year. He found he had missed
that shirt.

He read.

"Dear Bingo,"

Bingo leaned closer. He looked. He drew in a deep breath.

Melissa had underlined the word "Dear"! Then she had erased the underline, but Bingo could still see it! He was practically positive she had underlined "Dear." And an underlined "Dear" was the same as a "Dearest."

Bingo decided he would underline his, too, only he would not erase his. In his new manliness, he might even underline his twice, making it a "Dear Dearest"! Bingo felt he was just now beginning to understand the subtleties of his new language.

He glanced at Melissa's letter to him, then at his to her. He had so much to read, so much to write, he hardly knew where to begin.

And there were Triumphs to list! Real Triumphs! All in all, it had been a triumphant summer.

He had fallen out of love with Melissa, suffered, then discovered his suffering was in vain. He loved her more than ever.

He had been deserted by his mother, learned he was to become a brother and that his father was to become his mother. He had not fallen apart, as some people would, at discoveries of this nature.

He had received five letters from Melissa, had been caught in the kitchen and in the living room with Cici, and had handled the ensuing misunderstandings with considerable dignity.

Most important of all, he had learned to dog-paddle in

the mainstream of life. And, make no mistake about it, Bingo thought with a shudder of pleasure, that is exactly what this was.

With a smile, Bingo bent to read Melissa's letter.